A Short Walk To the *Other Side*

Short Stories

by

Matthew J. Pallamary

Mystic Ink Publishing

MATTHEW J. PALLAMARY

Mystic Ink Publishing
San Diego, CA
www.mysticinkpublishing.com

ISBN 10: 0615949487 (sc)
ISBN 13: 978-0615949482 (sc)
Printed in the United States of America
San Bernardino, California

This book is printed on acid-free paper made from 30% post-consumer waste recycled material.

Library of Congress Control Number: 2014900510

Book Jacket and Page Design: Matthew J. Pallamary/San Diego CA
Author's Photograph: Matthew J. Pallamary -- Gibbs Photo/Malibu CA

DEDICATION

This book is dedicated to Colleen Kennedy, Barnaby Conrad, Ken Reeth, Joan Oppenheimer, Eric Hart, Cork Milner, Chuck Champlin, Charles M. Schulz, and Ray Bradbury.

CONTENTS

INTRODUCTION

Who are we really?
What or where are the boundaries between what we believe to be real and what we imagine?

Ancient tribal cultures gave equal credence to dreams, visions, and their waking worlds, treating them all as different degrees of one and the same all-encompassing reality.

Do we in fact know ourselves or our *true* nature?

How many times have we reacted impulsively, only to regret our actions later, often with the apology, "I'm sorry, I'm not myself today," or "I don't know what got into me."

In these moments of intense feeling, if we are not ourselves, then who or what are we?

Where do we *really* live?

The fact that the question arises makes the "other" implicit within ourselves. What is this "other"? Duality? Plurality? Divided self? Are we possessed by something other than ourselves or are we in denial of our other selves because we find their behavior unacceptable?

Do we possess them or do they possess us?

This quandary became the theme of an old time radio show that started with: "Who knows what lurks in the hearts of men? The Shadow knows."

How well do we know our shadows as individuals and collectively? Better still, how well do our shadows know us?

Regardless of who is "running the show" at any point in space and time, every choice we make can change our life forever, along with the lives and destinies of others. A momentary lapse of attention while driving can cripple, maim, or bring swift and sudden death.

One moment of careless passion can leave you responsible for another life or bring the imminent end of your own from any number of ghastly diseases. A brief moment of passionate anger can land you in prison for the rest of your time on this earthly plane.

What doors do we pass through when we choose and what are the consequences of our actions? Better still, where do they leave us?

Coincidences, synergistic moments, timing, attitude, emotion, and attention can all change in the span of a single breath. What really goes on in the human heart and mind?

We cringe when we hear of, or witness heinous behavior and inhuman cruelty, yet human beings murder each other with endless and ingenious weapons of death, often in the name of a higher power.

Such disregard for life is difficult to comprehend, yet humans kill each other more than any other species. We are all human, so all of us are capable of making that one life altering choice that brings us someplace alien and unexpected.

Most people stay deeply entrenched in the cultural mainstream. Feeling safe and sane in their routines, they avoid those living on the fringes, believing that they could never sink so low and never think or act in such odd and terrifying ways, but we are all human, living within the same realm of possibilities. We all have our shadow selves. How much does it take to send us over the edge?

The truth is that it is a lot shorter walk to the other side than we like to think.

WRINKLE VILLAGE

Mary Anne first felt it with the cancer that insinuated itself into Grandma's body when she found Grandma's head drooping like a wilted flower, with eyes closed, breathing soft and shallow. One touch from Mary Anne made Grandma come alive, but it left Mary Anne feeling tired. She thought that she might be a healer, but as the cancer progressed, each time she enlivened Grandma with what Grandma called her "magic touch", Mary Anne paid the price with more exhaustion.

Seeing Mrs. Johnson in her wheelchair stirred those memories. She even looked like Grandma; white-haired and frail with milky blue eyes and trembling hands that felt dry and papery. If Mary Anne stretched her mind, the other residents of Willowbrook reminded her of Grandma too.

Silver-haired Mr. Wickers with his red flannel bathrobe, quivering legs, and gnarled hands. Mrs. Buckley, bitter and sharp featured, sneaking cigarettes every chance she could. Mr. Ford with his cards. Sherman Hamilton, the checker king.

Willowbrook. Mary Anne called it Wrinkle Village. She had been a nurse's aide for three weeks now and already felt attached to her patients.

"You're such an angel," Mrs. Johnson said, breaking in on Mary Anne's reverie. "A beautiful, blonde, blue-eyed angel."

Mary Anne felt her face flush. "Thank you, Mrs. Johnson." She wiped chicken soup from the old woman's chin. "Is there anything else I can get you?"

The old woman's eyes brightened when she patted Mary Anne's arm. "No thank you, dear. Just having you here is enough."

Mary Anne smiled and started to take the soup away when she felt a wave of dizziness.

"Are you all right, dear?"

Mary Anne looked up at Mrs. Johnson's bright blue eyes and demure smile. Her vision clouded. "I'm fine. A little tired, that's all. My shift's almost over. I'll go home and lie down for awhile."

Mrs. Johnson nodded. "Good idea."

Mary Anne made her rounds, checking the rest of her charges, then dragged herself home. After eating, she crawled into bed where sleep swallowed her, deep and dreamless.

*   *   *

Mr. Wickers and Mrs. Buckley greeted her the next morning in front of Willowbrook where they sat together among some other patients.

The weight of their expectant gazes made Mary Anne uneasy. She looked at the canes and walkers strewn among the lawn chairs. How long had some of them been here?

"Good morning," she said, pushing morbid thoughts from her mind. Most of them nodded. She stepped into the foyer and recognized Nurse Beckett's white hair and starched white uniform as she came out of the office. Gray eyes met Mary Anne's from behind steel-rimmed glasses. "Good, morning, dear. How are things going?"

"Great."

Nurse Beckett smiled her approval and moved off down the hall.

Mary Anne zipped through her morning duties, feeling light on her feet until she came across Mr. Wickers in the upstairs dayroom watching a soap opera with Mrs. Johnson.

"How are you today?" she said, pulling a chair up beside them. Sleepy eyes greeted her before brightening in delayed recognition.

"Oh, Mary Anne," Mrs. Johnson said in a reedy voice. "How lovely to see you." She smiled, baring yellowed dentures and placed a skeletal hand on Mary Anne's arm. "You're doing such a wonderful job. Isn't that so, Mr. Wickers?"

He twirled his mustache and nodded. "You bring life to a bunch of old fogies." He and Mrs. Johnson exchanged glances. Mary Anne opened her mouth and forgot what she was going to say. Mrs. Johnson became animated, her blue eyes flashing, voice cracking in a sing-song lilt about gardening, knitting, the latest soap operas, and the weather. Though the older woman spoke with boundless energy, Mary Anne could hardly keep her eyes open.

Each word felt like an added weight to her already faltering eyelids. She struggled, hearing phrases, yet unable to make sense of them. Excuse me." She stifled a yawn. "I have to get back to work."

*   *   *

Mary Anne crawled out of bed the following morning, feeling as if a flu had come over her during the night. After showering, she paused in front of the mirror. Her face looked haggard and for the first time in her life, she noticed tiny crow's feet at the corners of her eyes. I'm working way too hard, she thought. I need to pace myself.

After two cups of coffee, she headed for Willowbrook where she found Mr. Wickers and Mrs. Johnson out front in their usual place with the others. When Mary Anne saw them, she forced a smile and went into the building.

She recognized a slight furtive man with white hair and thin lips in the hall outside his office. Dr. Hunter spoke in a low, quiet voice. "You're doing a fine job," he said cheerfully. We're lucky to have you."

Mary Anne felt embarrassed. "Thank you, doctor."

"If there's anything you need, anything that troubles you, you come see me," he said.

She thanked him and hurried to the elevator. The smell of cigarette smoke came to her when the doors opened on the second floor. She followed it until she came across Mrs. Buckley sitting in the outdoor patio, a faded blue bathrobe hanging on her slender frame like rags on a skeleton. Her watery gray eyes looked washed out, reminding Mary Anne of the way she felt.

"Hi," she said, trying to sound cheerful.

Mrs. Buckley spasmed with a hacking cough. "You look a little pale," she rasped. "Come sit. We'll talk."

"I'd love to, but I have to finish..."

"You can spare a few minutes for an old biddy, can't you?"

Mrs. Buckley's gaze grew distant, then her eyes came back into focus. She rested a frail hand on Mary Anne's arm. "My memory's not what it used to be, but I do recall some things."

She spoke about her life, droning on, catching Mary Anne in her spell. Mary Anne fought to keep her drooping eyelids open, finally summoning all her strength to force herself up from the chair. She rushed out of the room, glancing back to apologize. Mrs. Buckley

13

smiled. Mary Anne grabbed at the door jamb, engulfed in a rush of lightheadedness.

She breathed in slow and deep, moving unsteadily down the corridor in search of Dr. Hunter. When she reached his office she paused to steady herself, then knocked.

"Come in," he said.

She found the doctor hunched over his desk writing. "With you in a moment," he muttered.

Mary Anne dropped into a chair.

Doctor Hunter looked up, a concerned frown creasing his forehead. "You all right?" He came around from behind his desk before she could answer. "Maybe you'd better lie down." He helped her out of the chair.

She stood on wobbly legs, allowing him to lead her to a couch. "When did this start?" he said.

"I'm sorry." She stifled a yawn. "I feel so tired. And dizzy. I must be working too hard. All I want to do is sleep."

Dr. Hunter leaned over her and placed a cool hand on her forehead. She drifted. "Sleep now," he said softly. "Get some rest."

She could barely hear him.

*　　　　*　　　　*

She awoke the following morning at home, unable to remember how she got there or how long she had slept. A vague memory of talking to Dr. Hunter flitted through her mind, but she couldn't recall their discussion. The more she struggled to remember, the further it slipped.

She moved around her apartment in a daze, putting things down, then forgetting where she left them. A sense of something being wrong sang through her like a muted klaxon. She hurried to Willowbrook, anxious to talk to Dr. Hunter.

As usual, Mrs. Buckley and Mr. Wickers sat out front, smiling and nodding their greetings. Inside, Nurse Beckett and Dr. Hunter met her in the hall.

"Good morning," he said. "Ready for another day?"

She stared at him, then at Nurse Beckett, expecting one of them to say something, but neither spoke.

Feeling embarrassed, Mary Anne hurried to the elevators.

Once upstairs, Mrs. Johnson asked her to sit and chat. Reluctantly, Mary Anne took a seat and let the old woman talk. As soon as she spoke, Mary Anne's eyelids felt heavier. "Excuse me." She forced herself to stand and stagger down to Dr. Hunter's office.

She caught her reflection in the hall mirror as she hurried by, thinking that her crow's feet looked more defined and her blue eyes had faded, looking gray and splotchy like blown fuses.

Panicking, she pushed her way into Dr. Hunter's office. The kind, welcome look on his face puzzled her. He came from behind his desk and hugged her. "Lie down here," he said, guiding her to the couch.

Something inside rebelled, but she dutifully followed his lead, yearning for the solace of sleep.

She reclined on the couch and instantly lost her sense of time, feeling dimly aware that much had passed. It could have been days, weeks, or months. She had no way of telling. She thought she was finally waking when she saw Dr. Hunter and Nurse Beckett leaning over her.

They looked younger and in an odd way she felt older. They had their hands on her. She strained to lift her head, but it felt like a bowling ball on the end of a thin branch.

Her breathing came shallow and her heart beat weaker. Her skin felt taut and dry like shrunken leather. She raised a trembling hand, touching it to chapped lips. Limp, silvery-gray hair spread beneath her on the pillow like faded mop strings. A tear rolled down the side of her face. She closed her eyes and escaped back into sleep.

*　　　　　*　　　　　*

Hillary was the new girl's name. So young and full of life.

"So, tell me, Miss Kennedy, how long have you been here?"

Mary Anne strained for a remnant of thought, but the answer slipped beyond her reach. She brushed gray hair from her eyes with a shaking hand and sighed, watching the young girl breeze through the room, red hair shining, green eyes flashing. She wanted so much to talk to her.

Touch her.

VICTIM OF LOVE

Footsteps and the clink clink of a belt buckle come to you in the darkness. Your breath catches and your hand under your pillow touches cold metal. You pull the covers up tighter to your chin and fake being asleep.

Clink. Clink.

Please God, No. You open one eye and peek at the door.

Silence.

He didn't go away. He won't until he uses it. He never brings it without using it. You wish he'd run in and get it over with, but he won't. He loves this part of the game.

You're wearing three pairs of pants and four shirts under your nightgown, but you know it's still going to hurt. How long will he make you wait this time? You stare at the crack in the door and think you see him glaring back at you, so you shut your eyes. Chills ripple up and down your spine.

The door creaks open and his footsteps come closer, stopping next to your bed. You feel his eyes on you, going up and down your body like two slimy hands, then the sound of his zipper.

"You can't fool me," he growls. "I know you're awake."

He pulls the covers from you and you roll onto your stomach, curling into a ball to protect yourself.

"Open up for Daddy like a little flower," he says.

The smell of alcohol sickens you. You curl up tighter, then it comes.

Thwack! Pain flashes across your backside, stinging. "No, Daddy," you whisper. "No." You grit your teeth and try not to cry. The buckle comes down again. Thwack!

"You can't hold out on me, you little bitch."

16

You bury your head in your arms and feel hot tears as the angry buckle bites into you, its frenzy increasing as Daddy punctuates his words with each strike.

"How," Whack "many times", Whack, "have I told you?" Whack. "Don't *ever*," Whack, "disobey me." Whack.

Your body jerks each time, jolted by electric pain. You clench your teeth harder, but the cries still escape, then you feel warmth spreading down your thighs. The final humiliation.

No sound but your sobs filling the room.

"Don't you know Daddy *loves* you?" His voice sounds like his mouth is full of syrup. You push your face into the pillow and your body squeezes tighter in anticipation of his touch. It makes you feel dirty.

"You don't think I *like* beating you, do you?" he whispers. Clammy, trembling hands touch your arms, then travel slowly down your back, lingering on your burning backside, then his hot, wet whiskey lips caress the back of your neck, wracking you with shivers. "I love you," he says softly.

You turn toward him and your hand slides over the metal under your pillow. You pull it out, pressing it to the side of Daddy's head. His eyes widen and his mouth drops.

"I love you too, Daddy."

You pull the trigger with both hands and your world explodes as the gun jumps -- again and again. Bang. Bang. Bang. Bang. Each thunderclap fills your ears and the acrid bite of gunpowder burns your nostrils. Daddy's blood spills on your bedspread when he falls on top of you, surprise frozen on his face.

Click. Click. Click. You keep squeezing. The weight of his body presses on you while his warm blood soaks through the sheets.

You run out into the backyard. Snow is falling. You take the gun and hide it under the back porch, then go inside to wait.

The police find you sitting in the front room, your face and nightgown splotched red. They find Daddy in your bedroom and want to know what happened. They ask questions, but you don't answer. First the police station, then the hospitals. More police. Psychiatrists. Courts. Months of the same people. Same places. Same questions. Same answers.

None.

Then one day a familiar face. Uncle Billy! You smile and run to his outstretched arms. He catches you and twirls you around. A flood of warm memories come rushing back. You, Daddy, and Uncle Billy. Before Mommy died. Before the drinking. Uncle Billy's house at

Christmas. New toys. Clothes.

"Hi, honey. You want to get out of this place and come live with me in your own room?"

On the way out of town, he stops at your old house. "No, Honey, you don't have to go in," he says. "I just want to get some of your things."

But you want to go. He lets you.

Soon you're making the long drive to Uncle Billy's. When you get there you're delighted to find your own room decorated in your favorite colors. Your heart fills with happiness as you pull the down comforter up to your chin. Contented, you begin drifting off to sleep when you hear footsteps and the clink clink of a belt buckle coming to you in the darkness. Your hand touches cold metal under your pillow.

WHEN MORE THAN ONE GATHER IN HER NAME

The front passenger tire popped and hissed, jerking the steering wheel in Margaux's hands. She fought it, holding tight so she could ease the van into a clearing off of a two-lane jungle road north of Belize.

Margaux shut the engine off after the van rolled to a stop and put her face in her hands, letting her tears fall in silence so she wouldn't wake little Jacob and Amanda who had miraculously slept through the blow out.

Outside, birds chattered and crickets sang in the surrounding jungle, announcing the approaching night. The warm humidity of the day would soon grow cool. No way could she change a tire in the dark by herself.

Margaux had driven all the way to Belize from San Diego only to be turned away at the border because she didn't have visas for Jacob and Amanda. The State Department had reassured her that visas for a two and three year old wouldn't be necessary.

Public servants, she thought, clenching her fists. Damn them!

"*No entrar,*" the black-haired federale with a thin mustache and mirrored glasses repeated at the check point. Margaux pleaded with him for forty-five minutes until he called two soldiers to enforce his point. She drove off before they reached her, but the damage had been done. She had no doubt that Jake would find out what happened and come looking.

Margaux gazed at the last red glimmer of sunlight over the tops of the trees. She had hoped to find a safe place for the night other than hotels. Like it or not she had one now. She sighed. Jake's eyes and ears would be everywhere. If he found her he would take Amanda and

Jacob.

Exhausted from driving jungle roads, Margaux closed her eyes and said a mental prayer. Her faith in truth and integrity had been shattered by a justice system manipulated by Jake's lies and money, but she still believed in the power of spirit over matter.

When she first met Jake he seemed like a carefree little boy who loved flying his airplanes, driving his sports cars, skiing, sailing, and scuba diving. Everything in life equated to fun until she had Amanda. When Jake lost his place as the center of Margaux's attention, an angry, spoiled Momma's boy burst to the surface like some undead creature from a horror movie. She should have known when he surprised her with a prenuptial agreement the day before their wedding.

"Mimi", her best friend Robin called him. "Everything is me me me. Don't do it, Margaux," she urged. "He's a snake."

On their honeymoon, when Jake shared his insecurities about growing up with no friends, she confided her drunk driving arrest after a sorority party and how she had smoked pot in the dorm.

Before they divorced, Jake deeded all of his properties over to his family and friends to make it look like he had no assets, then he used everything Margaux told him against her to make her look like an unfit mother. He took everything she had and kept coming for Jacob and Amanda.

A tap on the window made her jump. A lithe, brown- skinned Indian girl with silken black hair in a blue and white patterned poncho stood by the door with an armload of jewelry. Margaux looked past her, then in front and behind. No buildings or other signs of life. Where had she come from?

"*Hola*," Margaux said, rolling down the window.

The girl put something smooth and heavy in Margaux's hand, covering it with her own slender fingers. The deliberateness of the act stunned Margaux. She looked into the girl's open face and felt compassion coming from her dark almond shaped eyes. The girl smiled demurely and nodded toward Margaux's hand.

Looking down, Margaux saw a carved obsidian jaguar with finely detailed jaws, fangs, and feline eyes. Smooth muscles defined its thick forelegs. Olmec? Toltec? She couldn't tell.

"*Treinta pesos, señora,*" the Indian girl said. Though Margaux had less than a thousand pesos, the girl's eyes compelled her. As if reading Margaux's thoughts, she nodded toward the back of the van. "*El Tigre es la guardiána para sus niños.*"

20

Even though I really can't afford it, she'll probably feed her family for a week on this, Margaux thought, counting out the money.

"*Muchas gracias, señora.*" The joy that filled the girl's face sealed it.

"Mommy," Amanda said from the back of the van.

Margaux looked behind her into the fading light to see Amanda sitting up.

"Just a minute, Pumpkin."

She turned back to find the Indian girl gone. She checked the windows and rear view mirrors. Vanished.

"Mommy," Amanda said again. "Why are we stopped? Are we sleeping here tonight?"

Margaux stuffed the jaguar into her pocket, grabbed a flashlight and went to the back of the van where Amanda sat, her fluffy mane of disheveled blonde hair, mirroring her mother's. Margaux checked the rear window. The night jungle scared her, but the possibility of someone taking her babies from her in some Central American town frightened her more. Maybe this was a safer spot.

"Yes, we are," she said, sitting down beside her daughter. Amanda put her head in her mother's lap and fell asleep while Margaux stroked her hair. Darkness enveloped them and the songs of night birds and the chorus of crickets grew louder.

Easing Amanda from her lap, Margaux kissed her on the forehead and checked Jacob, whose breathing came slow and even. She kissed him on the cheek and stretched out at their feet. Feeling a bump in her hip, she pulled the jaguar from her pocket. The smooth black stone felt warm. What on earth had possessed her to buy it? She flicked on the flashlight and looked at it once again. Its fanged jaw and feline eyes seemed to smile.

Margaux clicked off the flashlight and closed her eyes, holding the figure, feeling strangely comforted by its warmth. She relaxed, listening to Amanda and Jacob's breathing, and drifted, lulled by their rhythm and the sounds of the jungle until she felt herself contracting, then rising as her awareness blossomed, filling the van, then the jungle around her, touching everything in it.

The throaty yowl of a huge cat captured her attention, its presence touching her as if no distance existed between them. The message made it unquestionably clear. The cat ruled all here.

Margaux twitched as if shocked. A clear picture of a beautiful, sleek, dignified black jaguar crouched behind a clump of bushes near the mouth of a cave filled her mind. Her body hummed and the vision felt visceral and direct, connecting Margaux with every cell of the jaguar's

21

body until she became the cat rather than observing it.

The mewling cries of her cubs made her ears stand straight. She sniffed the air at the cave entrance, sensing her babies and their fear intermingled with a cold presence that tensed her into hyper-awareness. Icy ripples shot down her spine, putting her hair on end. Her back arched.

Heart thumping, she moved into the cool darkness low to the ground; eyes, ears, and nose all focused on the danger she knew awaited her. A few more steps and she spotted her trembling babies cornered by a huge Anaconda, jaws wide, its thick body coiled to strike.

She leaped, catching the snake's neck with her teeth when it turned to strike at her. Its slithering body found hers, sending both of them tumbling to the ground. The snake squeezed, constricting and shutting down her breath while she bit, clawed, and slashed with full fury. Her awareness shrank to darkness until she gnawed through the snake's neck. The suffocating pressure faltered and fell slack, rewarding her with the sweetness of the Anaconda's fluid essence.

She extricated herself from the serpentine prison and caught her breath before biting and clawing more, shredding the snake, giving two portions to her hungry babies before finishing the rest herself.

When the last of the meat had been eaten, Margaux's perceptions grew fuzzy, coming back into focus still with the jaguar, realizing that she had shared a memory and an understanding that bonded them. As long as she lived, nothing would take her babies from her.

She saw the van through the trees ahead. Picking up her pace, she covered the distance in several leaps, ending with one big one that sent her bounding through the passenger window. On entering, she felt a dizzying shift that brought her back to her sleeping self at the same time the jaguar came through the window.

The cat paced back and forth, approaching Margaux cautiously. Though separate, the powerful energetic connection remained between them. If Margaux moved or had aggressive thoughts or feelings, she sensed a shift in their connection that could cause the cat to bolt at any second. Feeling equal parts fear and respect, Margaux knew she would be safe in the jaguar's presence as long as she maintained her state of mind, which was simply to learn without thinking.

The jag stopped a couple of inches away, looked directly at Margaux and tensed every muscle in its body. She stared, unblinking, and it seemed to Margaux that the jaguar's eyes touched her very soul. Margaux shuddered, imagining the cat shredding her the way it had the snake. The jaguar thrust its neck forward, bared its teeth and hissed.

When it stopped, Margaux flooded with love and appreciation. No longer fearful, she found herself in awe of the jag. It lay down, groomed itself and gazed past Margaux as if it didn't matter whether she was there or not. A rumbling sound came from somewhere deep inside of it. It took Margaux a moment to realize that the jaguar purred like a house cat, except with greater volume; a deep rumbling tone that resonated in the trunk of Margaux's body in an almost sexual way.

In that moment, Margaux received a new perspective on boundaries and territories as well as a reverence for hunting and a deep, sacred respect and love for the spirit of prey. The jaguar had a profound understanding of nature and related to it as an awesome force within which every intelligence took part, be they hunter, hunted, or other form of life.

Margaux closed her eyes and they continued communicating in what she could only think of as rapid telepathic thought-emotion exchanges. Her forceful responses were answered by the jaguar, firmly asserting its place as the unquestioned teacher until every thought and response played itself out to its logical end.

In spite of the truth and profundity of the lessons, Margaux doubted what she experienced, so she closed her eyes and asked with her mind, "If this is really happening and we are connected, can you show me a sign? I'm not trying to assert my will or tell you what to do, I'm only looking for a sign."

Something soft touched Margaux's ankle. The jaguar put its head down and ran the side of her face up and down Margaux's leg as if marking Margaux as hers. She sidled alongside Margaux until her nose touched Margaux's cheek, then she backed off.

Amazement overcame Margaux's doubt and she sat up. Keeping the connection in her head, she looked to the jaguar. Their eyes connected and merged. Margaux held her hand out in what she thought of as a submissive gesture and the jaguar pawed and nipped at it with sheathed claws and gentle bites, as if testing and proving she was still in charge. Margaux remained fearless and neutral, determined to be unshaken in her openness, surrendering while being neither passive nor aggressive. The cat took Margaux's hand in its paws and licked her fingertips with tiny languishing flicks of her tongue that Margaux thought of as kitty licks. Margaux understood this to be the jaguar's own gesture of submission.

As quickly as she had come, the jaguar hopped to her feet and turned away as if her old stand-offish self had come back to make sure

Margaux didn't forget who was boss.

The van shook and the jaguar hopped out through the passenger window. Margaux sat up blinking, marveling at how real it had seemed. She felt her hand and fingers. Wet.

Confusion enveloped her when she saw lights, then the driver's door opened and Jake climbed in, a hateful expression contorting his face. Margaux felt the weight of the stone figure in her hand. Outside, the throaty yowl of a jaguar captured her awareness, its presence touching her, reminding her that no distance existed between them.

UNREQUITED LOVE

The infant's mouth opened in anguished protest at its entrance into the world before life rushed in, filling its lungs with precious air. Hearing no sound and thinking that the baby couldn't breathe, the doctor slapped its back side with increasing vigor until he saw the infant's stomach pumping in and out. Its mouth made all the movements of crying without so much as a whisper.

As the child grew, his cognizance and comprehension blossomed. Reality came to him in vivid color and its sounds rang clear and full of a wonder that stirred deep longings which he yearned to express, but when he opened his mouth to do so, only the hiss of his breath came forth.

He had come into this world without the means to vocalize, but his mute state had no effect on his developing mind. If anything, it enhanced it. What he lacked in articulation had been more than compensated for with a sharp and apprehensive mind.

Intelligence shone in his eyes whenever he encountered something new, stimulating his infant fascination. As he continued to grow, his curiosity took in the world like a sophisticated intelligence gathering machine from another planet.

Given one or two details, he could fathom the remaining pieces of almost any puzzle, but his inner life raged with pent-up feelings that he could not emote, frustrating him every time he attempted to convey his inner life. His unreleased feelings grew stronger with each eruption, but his developing emotions could only be acted out in animated silence.

Only music placated him.

When the pain of his unarticulated passion became more than he could bear, he played his music loud, finding comfort by pressing his ear to the speaker so he could not only hear, but he could feel; assimilating the sweet sounds of aural desire into the depths of himself, making them his own.

Other forms of expression affected him just as deeply. Delicately rendered pictures brought tears to his eyes and the joy and thrill of beautiful harmonies lifted his heart, but he treasured words more than anything else. The enunciations of thought and feeling he could not speak held a magic he could never experience.

Day after day, he sat staring out the front window, listening to the screams and cries of kids playing in the street, cut off from their talking, sharing and arguing. He felt so distant, their presence made him feel alien. He would have given anything to be part of their world. Anything to make contact. Share. Communicate. Connect.

Each day he gazed out the window, longing to touch the lives of those who passed, feeling the distance between his world and theirs as an abyss that he could never cross; until the warm summer day that she passed beneath his window. Dark haired, she had hazel eyes, an angelic face, and the sweetest smile he had ever seen. The instant their eyes met, his empty heart imploded. She gazed back at him in that timeless moment, sending a bolt of recognition shooting through him.

His whole being expanded beyond the boundaries of his self, losing control as it lost itself in the depths of her eyes. She smiled and he realized that he smiled too. Reaching toward her, he pressed his fingertips to the window, longing to touch...

He heard voices and saw others coming down the street. She kept looking, smiling as if they did not exist. His mouth worked from side to side in a silent parody of speech as every fiber of his being strained to articulate his love. She frowned at his actions and a hurt look pinched her beautiful features, then someone in the passing crowd pointed at him and laughed.

He cried out, mouth wide in tortured silence as others joined in the laughter. His body tightened, first with pain, then rage. Every part of him shook down to the core of his essence until a tingle surged through him, rising in intensity, burgeoning until his fingertips buzzed against the window. The glass beneath them started to hum and the hum grew louder.

The laughter stopped and the hum crescendoed into a tortured wail that pierced the hearts of all who heard it, holding nothing back as it gave all of itself to this moment of pure expression. The air around him erupted in silvery green light that spiderwebbed into a shimmering sphere, then the ball brightened like a rising flame before exploding in a brilliant shower of silent sparks that trailed into nothingness, leaving nothing but shattered glass as testimony that he had ever been a part of this world.

COLLECTOR'S ITEM

NANCY

AN ORIGINAL ADDITION TO THE CHILDREN-OF-THE-WORLD COLLECTION CREATED BY THE WORLD-RENOWNED ROBOTIC DOLLMAKER HANS HESSMAN.

"Sugar and spice and everything nice."

Little Nancy is all that and more. Blue eyed with golden hair and a bright little girl smile. Standing three feet tall she's cute as a button dressed in her pink organdy dress. Her expressive face, detailed costume, authentic vocalizations, and realistic movements clearly establish her as a one of a kind doll.

Collectors will note her lifelike eyes and tender, baby soft skin that have become the trademark of Mr. Hessman, who has once again demonstrated his consummate artistic engineering skills in the creation of little Nancy Garrett.

You can actually feel her warmth.

Ginny put down the placard and ran her slender fingers through Nancy's hair, resting them briefly on the doll's bare shoulder before pulling her hand away.

It *did* feel warm.

She shifted her handbag to her other shoulder, then read on.

> Hans Hessman's work as a doll maker is known to top tier animatronic doll collectors throughout the world. He has won more than sixty prizes for his creations in major, juried exhibitions. Coming from a long line of engineers, which go all the way back to the impeccable craftsmanship of early German watch makers, Mr. Hessman emigrated to the United States from Germany as a child in the mid-twentieth century and has worked at perfecting the skills passed on to him through generations ever since. His unique creations have been critically acclaimed for their realism and sculptural excellence.
>
> Like the rest of Mr. Hessman's creations, Nancy is unique, making her a collector's item. She comes complete with a birth certificate endorsed by Mr. Hessman.

Ginny put the placard down and studied the doll, her own hazel eyes transfixed by the blue gaze of the doll.

"I only put her out this morning," a deep female voice said.

Ginny looked up, and saw a plump, gray-haired older woman waddling through the Fifth Avenue gallery toward her.

"She looks so real," Ginny said. "and so cute." She stood back admiring the doll.

"Almost *too* real." The woman tilted her head to the side and studied Little Nancy for a moment, then she reached behind its head and gently squeezed its neck. Little Nancy blinked as if waking from a trance. Her mouth turned up in an adorable smile.

"Hi, are you my Mommy?" She said in a sweet diminutive voice. Her little eyelids fluttered.

Ginny gasped, then sighed. "She's adorable."

The woman nodded. "It's a Hessman original. He's getting old. I don't think he'll be producing many more."

Ginny rubbed the doll's arm. "It feels so real. And the detail.

Right down to the tiny hairs on its arms. She's absolutely beautiful."

"She won't be here long," the old woman said. "Hessman's work always goes quickly."

Ginny looked back at the doll, once more marveling at its loving expression. "How much?"

"Sixty thousand."

Ginny pulled her credit card from her wallet in her purse.

*   *   *

Before going to bed that night, Ginny stood Nancy in the corner of her bedroom below a picture of her husband and daughter. She gazed at the picture a moment, then kissed her finger and pressed it to the glass.

"Nobody wants to talk about them anymore," she said half to herself and half to the doll. "They think I should put them behind me, but I can't. I'm so lonely without them."

She turned her attention to the doll.

"There, Honey." She rested her hand on Nancy's cheek, then slid it around to the back of the doll's head and gently squeezed her neck. "I used to have a little girl like you. She's gone, but now I have you."

Little Nancy blinked and in her soft childlike voice said, "Don't be sad, Mommy. I'm your little girl now. I'll love you forever, no matter what!"

Ginny felt tears welling in her eyes. "Neither of us will have to be alone anymore," she said through shaky breath.

The smoothness of Little Nancy's skin, combined with its velvety warmth sent a rush of emotion through Ginny. She pulled the doll to her breast and hugged it. Its whole body had the same subtle warmth. She held it at arm's length for a moment before kissing it on the forehead and setting it down in the corner, then she pulled out the birth certificate and crawled into bed. Sitting cross-legged with pillows propped up behind her, she read.

Name: NANCY GARRETT

Date of birth: JUNE 21, 2014

Delivering physician: HANS HESSMAN

A picture of a frail, white-haired old man sitting with the doll on his lap was in the upper right corner of the certificate. Hans Hessman's signature appeared on the bottom line next to the title of delivering physician.

Ginny put the certificate on her night stand, winked at Nancy, then turned out the light and went to sleep.

*   *   *

Something woke Ginny.

She rolled over in bed, her eyes locking with Nancy's. A pale yellow streetlight shone through the window, framing the doll's eyes in a tiny rectangle of orange light, causing them to sparkle.

It looks like she's crying, Ginny thought.

Little Nancy's hands extended out as though reaching to be picked up. Ginny turned her back to the doll and pulled the covers up over her shoulder, staying awake for a long time, telling herself that she didn't feel the tingle crawling down the nape of her neck. Eventually she drifted, sliding somewhere between sleep and waking.

"Help! Mommy, mommy, don't let them take me."

The voice sounded distant at first. Then louder. "Mommy, they're taking me!"

Ginny sat up straight, rubbing her eyes. The light from the window no longer framed Nancy's eyes. In the corner, the doll's hands spread wide, its face looked contorted in terror, its mouth open as if screaming. Ginny rubbed her eyes again and fumbled for the light switch.

In the sudden glare, she saw Nancy standing just as she'd left her. Taking deep breaths, she calmed herself, letting sleep come once again.

"Help! Mommy, mommy, they're taking me!"

Ginny watched in horror as two burly men threw a blanket over the little blonde girl and tossed her into a van. A muffled scream came from its confines before the side door slid shut, cutting off the sound.

"Somebody stop them!"

Her own scream woke her. She sat up, wiping tears from her eyes. Little Nancy lay on her side, hands drawn up toward her face.

"Oh baby, Honey." Ginny stretched out on the floor beside the doll. "What happened to you?" She stroked Nancy's baby soft blonde hair and peered into her glistening eyes. She wanted to touch them to see if they were really wet, but couldn't bear the thought of finding out. Instead, she draped her arm over Nancy and softly cried herself to sleep.

*　　　　　　*　　　　　　*

She awoke the following morning in bed. Bright sunlight streamed in through the window. The doll stood by itself in the corner, looking exactly as it had when she brought it home.

What's happening? She thought.

She got up, went to Nancy and ran her fingers over the plush carpet where she remembered laying her head.

It felt damp.

*　　　　　　*　　　　　　*

"I'm telling you, there's something strange about this doll." Ginny moved the phone to her other shoulder as she poured her tea.

"What do you mean?" The woman from the gallery said.

"I don't know. It's just that, well – it's – it's *too* lifelike."

"Are you feeling all right? If it's that upsetting, you can always return it. We don't want any unsatisfied customers."

Ginny felt her face flush. "I'm fine." She ended the call, put her cell phone down, and walked over to the refrigerator where she took out a carton of milk. After pouring a splash into her cup, she stared at the back of the carton. Her cup slipped from her fingers and fell to the floor, shattering. "My God!" She cried, seeing little Nancy's picture on the back of it.

MISSING SINCE JUNE 21, 2013

NANCY JONES

HAIR: BLONDE   EYES: BLUE

DATE OF BIRTH: 11 - 12 - 2009

LAST SEEN WEARING A PINK ORGANDY DRESS.

Ginny ran from the kitchen, stumbled upstairs, and into her bedroom.

Nancy was gone.

Ginny stumbled back down stairs in confusion and found a bottle of scotch. Unable to think, act, or make any decisions, she quickly downed a couple of shots and continued to drink herself into a stupor, numbing her paralysis until she drifted into deep alcoholic unconsciousness.

$*$ $*$ $*$

Still intoxicated late the following evening, Ginny stared at her cell phone on the kitchen table while clutching the milk carton. A newspaper lay on the table before her. Should she call? No! If Nancy came back, they'd take her away. She couldn't bear the thought of losing her baby again. She sobbed, pulled a handkerchief from her purse, and looked down at the tear-stained newspaper, her gaze coming to rest on a small article at the top of the page.

ROBOTIC ENGINEER BUTCHERED IN BIZARRE STABBING INCIDENT

The mutilated body of renowned animatronic doll maker Hans Hessman was found this morning by his maid, stabbed repeatedly from head to toe. Police have no leads. Highly respected for both his engineering and artistic skills, Hessman, known for his reclusiveness and dedication to his craft has been lauded worldwide for the impeccable craftsmanship that goes into his lifelike creations.

With no known enemies, police are questioning his associates for any information or possible motives for his grizzly death.

See **HESSMAN**, *page 3*

A sound from upstairs startled her. She jumped from her chair and ran up the stairs, stopping in the doorway of her darkened bedroom.

Nancy stood in the corner.

Ginny put her fist to her mouth and bit down hard as she stepped into the room. She took a deep breath and flicked on the light. Nancy's blue eyes sparkled and her perpetual little girl's smile spread wide on her face.

Ginny froze when she saw reddish-brown droplets of blood spattered across the front of Nancy's pink organdy dress.

THE EDGE

Holding a scalpel with sweaty fingers, Jacques watched the girl's breasts rise and fall with her gentle breathing. His gaze moved to her beautiful face which neared perfection -- but not quite.

He took a deep breath and brought the blade closer, savoring the shiver of anticipation that passed through him, then he sliced a graceful arc under her jaw. A line of blood welled up exposing fatty tissue. After two more quick cuts, he pulled at a flap of skin, rearranging it to highlight the curves and angles of her face.

Jacques took pride in being a sought after artist whose brushes were blades, his canvas, human flesh. Young, wealthy, wannabe starlets, celebutantes, and fading beauties clinging desperately to their diminishing youth all came to him, eager to submit to his blade. Every magical stroke of his scalpel changed destinies.

Jacques' art allowed the facade of their outer beauty to hide the truth of their distorted inner lives which he resented, particularly their hypocrisy, but he reveled in their worship and the knowledge that the magic wand that was his scalpel brought them happiness.

Perfection. His gift to his devoted scalpel slaves. Could you take this bump out of my nose? Highlight my cheekbones? Get rid of those crow's feet around my eyes? I'd like my breasts firmer. I have a little sag here. Can you take it in?

He made more cuts, nipping and tucking until his patient's face assumed prefect proportions, then he put in the last stitch, letting a nurse finish the dressing so he could rest.

The demands of those anxious for his gifts had grown rapidly, bringing him to the point where the exhilaration and letdown of each operation left him more drained than the one preceding it. Raising his

fees had only increased the demand, forcing him to extend his hours.

Jacques rubbed at his burning eyes and stretched out on his office couch, thinking of how many, with their own versions of flawed anatomy demanded his time and energy, and for the first time in his career, he worried about keeping up the relentless pace that drove him. Letting his weariness settle over him, he dozed, until a knock on the door startled him awake.

"Your next patient is prepped and ready," one of his nurses said.

Jacques sighed. "Be right there." Gathering his dwindling energies, he struggled to his feet, feeling the rising anticipation of another scalpel stroke.

He finished his last rhinoplasty some time after eight that night. Feeling drained, he wanted only to eat and sleep. Stopping for a quiet dinner on the way home, he almost bumped into a tall, silver-haired man in a tuxedo on the way into the restaurant. "Dr. Forsythe," Jacques blurted, extending his hand.

Forsythe shook it vigorously.

Jacques gestured toward the entrance. "Join me for a drink?"

Forsythe glanced at his watch. "I can spare a few minutes."

Jacques followed him in, waving to the hostess.

"Haven't seen you at the club in months," Forsythe said after the hostess seated them. "You feeling okay?" He leaned toward Jacques, a concerned look on his face. "You look like hell."

Jacques sighed. "Too many patients."

"Why do you push yourself so hard? You don't need the money."

"They need me," Jacques said, lowering his voice, "but they're sucking the life out of me."

Forsythe's eyes darted from side to side, then he looked over his shoulder. His mannerisms made Jacques uneasy.

"For the short term," Forsythe said after checking over his shoulder again, "you can extend yourself." He held his arm out and looked at his watch. "Gotta go." He pulled a small bottle from his pocket, winked and pressed it into Jacques's hand.

Jacques turned it over in his palm to read the label.

DEXEDRINE
Not to exceed six in a twenty four hour period.

The name on the label said "John Smith".

Forsythe disappeared before Jacques could respond, so he dropped the bottle into his jacket pocket and forgot about it.

*   *   *

The buzz of his alarm crashed through Jacques's skull the next morning, waking him in confused panic. After slapping the button, silence filled the room, leaving him with a throbbing headache.

Easing himself out of bed, he made his way to the bathroom, where he fumbled inside the medicine chest for some aspirin.

He felt better after showering, but the pounding in his head persisted. He wished he could take the day off, but he had twelve patients scheduled for surgery. Postponement would only jam his already overloaded schedule.

He slipped his hand into his pocket after shrugging into his jacket and felt the bottle. Forsythe's words came to mind. "For the short term, you can extend yourself."

He pushed the thought from his mind.

Losing himself in the morning's parade of facelifts and nose jobs, he concentrated on his art, but by the third patient his hands shook. He finished without incident, but what little energy he had mustered that morning had already dwindled.

Turning from the operating table, he held his hands in front of himself to stop the trembling, but his body wouldn't obey. He couldn't face another operation. Today his patients seemed to drain him faster than he could recharge.

He went into his office and pulled the Dexedrine from his pocket. Maybe just this once. For the short term. The weekend was coming and he could rest up then. He shook two pills from the bottle, washed them down with a cup of water and laid back on his couch.

His headache cleared as if strong winds had blown back thunderheads. His heartbeat came to life, thumping in his chest. His mind felt razor sharp, his energy boundless. His perceptions had a clarity he hadn't thought possible, and his hands felt firm.

Working through his patients, his fingers moved quickly, his every cut a stroke of excellence that brought each trusting face closer to perfection. A giddy sense of power rushed through him as he accented lines, angles, and highlights. His edge had returned.

Jacques left the office feeling euphoric, but by the time he reached home, his nerves felt like overstretched rubber bands. His mind still raced. He treated himself to Mozart and cognac.

He went to bed after two, drifting off into a troubled sleep. The next morning his limbs felt heavy, his thoughts disjointed. He pulled out the Dexedrine.

After two pills, his energy returned and his cuts stayed perfect. He worked his patients with flair and precision. That night he unwound with Beethoven and more cognac, priming himself the next morning once again with Dexedrine. By Friday he managed to reduce his stream of clients to a reasonable flow by persuading some to reschedule.

He knew where this would inevitably lead him so on Saturday morning he flushed the last of the Dexedrine down the toilet, but by Saturday afternoon he broke into a cold sweat and his body shook. Cravings gnawed at him. He tried escaping into sleep, but his discomfort kept him from anything more than an uneasy doze.

When he could bear his suffering no longer, he rummaged through his briefcase for a prescription pad. He didn't like the thought of drug dependence, but he was a doctor and felt confident that he could beat any addictive tendencies by counteracting one drug with another. He scribbled out two prescriptions; one for Dexedrine, one for Valium.

During the next few weeks, he performed his usual precision work with the aid of Dexedrine during the day and Valium at night to help him sleep. He kept his edge the first week, but it dulled some by Wednesday of the second, forcing him to increase the dosage.

By the third week his patient's features looked different, both before and after he made his cuts. He feared he was losing his touch.

By the fourth week his energy fluctuated, confirming his growing suspicion that his patients robbed him of his life substance, and as more time passed he found himself puzzling over his work. No matter what he did, nothing looked right to him, but no one complained.

Determined to clear his thoughts, Jacques took much needed time off and locked himself in the house with a supply of food and a variety of drugs, but his body had other ideas.

Chills, vomiting, and diarrhea wracked him soon after he decreased the dosage and in his state of extreme withdrawal, the radio played satanic music nonstop – even with the cord unplugged, then a gibbering woman with an ugly distorted face crawled through the screen of his television, ordering him to make her perfect.

Her ranting angered him. He couldn't let patients treat him this way. He was the one who controlled destinies, not them. He knew what he had to do if he wanted to regain his edge, so he applied his will and after a bitter struggle, he reclaimed his clarity and his edge returned.

Anxious to reassert his mastery, Jacques arrived at the clinic early the following morning as scheduled. His nurses prepped his first patient as he donned his gown and checked his operating schedule.

"Scalpel," he said a few minutes after the anesthesiologist put his first patient under. He stared at the blade, admiring the precision of its edge, then he glanced down at his unconscious patient's face. Her eyes opened and the woman who had crawled out of his television shouted, "Make me perfect!"

He looked at his nurse and anesthesiologist. Neither of them seemed to notice. He brought the blade closer and stopped when he saw another face. This one stayed quiet and kept her eyes closed. Her beauty looked nearly perfect until her features shifted again.

No matter.

Savoring the anticipation of his first stroke a moment longer, Jacques cut deep, exposing the fatty tissue underneath. The television lady smiled and winked at him. He smiled back. This one would be his greatest work of art.

NIGHT WHISPERS

Her beautiful white flowers called to me like silken bells. I couldn't resist the thrill she promised, so I went to her. Carlos said she could give me the gift of flight – and flying is what I wanted. Away from myself. Away from the hell that was my life.

I took the whole plant, chopping leaves, seeds, flowers, stems, and roots into a mixture that I boiled, adding honey to help its unpleasant taste, then I climbed into bed to wait for her. She came for me a short while later in a strong, sudden breeze that swept up everything in its path until I too was whisked away, taking flight, letting her carry me both upward and outward on her wings…

…until I awoke with a jolt, heart hammering, adrenaline pumping.
What the hell was that?
Sitting up, I took a deep breath.
Down in the cellar.
I swung my feet over the edge of the bed and stood, torn between the desire to investigate and the urge to run until I felt it coming toward me again like a cat stalking a sparrow. I shivered, waiting for it to pounce, but it only whispered in a multitude of voices, barely audible at first, then rising in volume, until they boomed through me.

Laughing, sighing, wailing -- with a familiarity that hung just beyond the reach of my awareness. Calling. *Drawing me* down to the cellar. I left the bedroom, heading for the kitchen at the end of the hall until I stopped at the top of the cellar stairs. They beckoned with greater urgency.

A faint blue light shimmered beneath the door, throbbing with the heartbeat that pounded in my ears. Nostalgia enveloped me and the voices rushed through me again like the wind passing over reeds in a pond, rattling them in its wake. Mom, Dad, Grandma, Joey.

A combination of fear, awe, and exhilaration overwhelmed me. Stumbling across the kitchen, I lunged toward the door until my hand found the knob, then I froze, unable to take another step.

Something rose up deep within me, confronting the obsession of the voices, canceling them out until they returned -- stronger. The power inside me rallied, and the voices came again, repeating the exchange over and over, each force confronting the other with increasing rapidity, until my mind raced aimlessly.

I turned the knob and pushed.

The dank smell of mildew assaulted me, then the door swung noiselessly on its hinges as though pulled by an unseen force.

They were all there, glowing in eerie fluttering bluish-green detail, like the aurora borealis; translucent, yet solid. Gesturing for me to join them. Their mouths moved as they spoke, but no words came. The cold trickle down the small of my back and the prickling sensation that danced across my scalp were the last physical sensations I remembered.

Like stepping off a cliff, I plummeted through the otherworldly colors into a dark abyss. My hands flew out, desperate for something solid, but I only twisted, tumbled, and screamed as the darkness claimed me for its own.

*   *   *

I opened my eyes back in my bedroom. The feeble light of the approaching day filtered in through the curtains, making my disheveled bed barely visible in the gray, predawn shadows. Leaning over it, I gazed into my eyes, wide in lifeless terror, and my mouth -- gaping in its own silent scream.

CHANGING CHANNELS

Kevin Lovelace plodded listlessly through the streets of San Diego; a tattered, bearded shell of the person his mother had spoiled as a baby. One minute he loved her, the next he hated her. The more he tried to figure out the way she made him feel, the more confused he became. Ever since his thirteenth birthday, when she said she loved him, he craved her attention more than anything, and she had always been more than generous in giving it, but after his party when they were alone, she started kissing him differently, then she touched him in a new way that felt good and made him feel bad at the same time.

From his loss of virginity, through all of his adult life, her love was the only love he ever knew, until he met a girl his own age a few days before his thirtieth birthday. When Mom found out, she broke all the dishes, then apologized and made a special cake for his birthday. When he didn't want to kiss her and do the other things, she exploded.

Since then, the girl had gone away and Kevin began to drift, moving from shelter to shelter, reduced to washing car windows and begging for spare change.

He didn't know how much longer he could...

The sound of a man's deep, resonating, wail pulled him from his reverie. He looked around until he saw dirt-streaked windows and peeling, forest green paint. The words painted on the run down storefront window caught his eye.

THE DIVINE LIGHT SPIRITUALIST CHURCH

Normally he wouldn't have noticed the gathering, but on this hot, humid night, the doors were open. A heavy-set man with dark skin, a round face, and a broad, flat nose sat in front of the congregation on a raised wooden platform, swaying rhythmically from side to side making a sound from deep in his throat that fell somewhere between a chant and a moan. He had jutting brows, dark curly hair, and wore a sky blue satin robe. A crystal on a heavy gold chain hung from his neck.

Kevin eased his way to the edge of the door and peered inside, standing on his tip-toes to see over the heads of the crowd. About twenty five people watched in rapt silence as the man said something about Atlantis and past lives, before stopping mid-sentence. He turned his head to one side as though listening, then his half-lidded eyes opened wide and locked on Kevin, holding the younger man's attention the way a cobra holds a rodent's before striking. "You!" the man said. His voice boomed and his head bobbed like a slow-moving pigeon's. "You are one of us."

I am? Kevin thought. What the hell is this guy talking about? I'm getting out of here. He turned to leave, but the voice stopped him.

"You have the gift. Come, join us."

The crowd turned and stared at Kevin. Driven forward by an inexplicable urge, he shuffled to the front of the room and took a seat by the edge of the platform. The heavy-set man smiled dreamily, then turned back to the congregation, who stood and applauded. The dark man on stage blinked and his expression changed as though passing from sleep to waking. He gestured toward Kevin, then turned and bowed to the crowd.

The service had ended.

The gathering applauded again and began a slow exodus from the "church". A few came up and spoke briefly with their leader, giving quick, furtive glances at Kevin before hurrying out, whispering to each other. Kevin felt awkward and got up to leave, but the man raised a meaty hand, stopping him.

"I'll be with you in a moment," he said quietly.

"Oh... Okay." Kevin sat down.

When the last of the crowd had gone, the man closed and locked the door, then turned and faced Kevin. The way the man locked the door made him nervous.

"Don't be alarmed," the man said as though reading his mind. "It's only a precaution to keep out undesirable elements."

"Why did you pick me out of the crowd like that?"

The man strode toward the stage. "I didn't. You picked me."

Kevin felt a wave of confusion. "I don't understand."

"What made you come in?"

"I don't know. Curiosity I guess."

"It was more than curiosity." The man pursed his thick lips, then relaxed, his expression becoming warm and friendly. "My name's Reverend Stevenson." He extended a large hand. "Nicholas to my friends."

"I'm Kevin." He stood and shook hands with the big man.

"I know you possess the gift," Nicholas said cryptically.

"What gift is that?"

Stevenson's doleful brown eyes stared at Kevin for a long uneasy moment as though boring into some secret part of his mind. "You have heard them, haven't you?"

"Heard them?"

"Your friends."

"How did you know?" Kevin said, his voice trembling.

He first became aware of them a few nights after his thirteenth birthday. He remembered waking in the middle of the night, jumping when he first heard the voices. They whispered, barely audible at first, then they rose in volume until they boomed through him and at him.

He listened to them long into the night, until his mother found him sitting by himself talking to no one as the first rays of sunlight streamed through his bedroom window.

After that first night, Kevin spent hours carrying on long conversations with them. When his mother took him in for treatment, Kevin's dialogue with them stopped. Relieved, his mother carried on with their lives as though nothing had happened. She didn't know that his friends still talked to him, only they did it in secret.

"I can sense it," the reverend said.

Kevin jumped at the sound of the priest's voice.

"The friends you and I hear are spirits," the priest continued. "They guide us. I allow mine to speak through me, as you've seen."

Kevin put his hands in his pockets and stared at the floor. "I only hear mine in my head."

"That's because you haven't learned how to channel them *through* you. I can teach you. Together we can build this humble congregation into a great one."

The voices of Kevin's friends rushed into his mind like wind-blown leaves filling a vacuum, urging him on. *You have been chosen by the Lord. Claim your destiny. Rise above the crowd. You will become a conduit for the Lord's will.*

A warm feeling swept over him, then the voices stopped as if a strong breeze slammed a door shut. Kevin looked up. His mind felt clear, awake and aware for the first time in a long time. He felt a smile creep across his face. "What do I have to do?"

"You can stay with me here," Nicholas said. "We'll get you some new clothes. Clean you up a bit."

*   *   *

Kevin finished off his second helping of fried chicken while Nicholas continued studying him, a faraway look in his eyes. Kevin let his own gaze wander, taking in his surroundings. The apartment above the storefront looked small and dingy, the wallpaper faded and yellowed. Grease spattered the kitchen walls and the air had a sour smell to it, but there was an extra room in the back. This apartment would do for now, besides, anything beat another night on the streets.

"For the first couple of weeks," Nicholas said, as his eyes came back into focus. "Simply come to the services and watch how the spirits come through me. Once you become familiar with their presence, one of them will choose you."

"Sure," Kevin said, thinking only of the fullness in his stomach. This guy's a strange bird, but if I play the game and go along with him…

He helped himself to another piece of chicken. Life could be very good. "How will I know when they choose me?"

"Don't worry. When the time is right, you will know."

*   *   *

After a month of attending services, a new wardrobe, a new haircut and shave, Nicholas told Kevin that he thought him ready to be called upon by the spirits of the church. By this time, Kevin thought for sure that the older man was more than a little crazy, but if he could act the way Nicholas did, he was sure that love, money, and power would come.

That night after services, when the last of the faithful had gone and the door was locked, Nicholas dimmed the lights and sat Kevin on a chair, center stage. "Watch the light glinting off my pendant." Nicholas dangled his crystal in front of Kevin's eyes. "And listen to my voice." He began a series of rhythmic chants. "Relax," Nicholas said softly. "Don't fight. Let me into your mind. Let us become one."

Kevin sighed, letting his shoulders sag. Nicholas was serious. Best play the game. By now he had seen Nicholas do this a bunch of times. He knew what to do. Letting his eyelids droop, he blinked once, twice, then closed them.

Nicholas leaned forward and lowered his voice. "From now on you will follow my instructions and allow what lies within to come forth -- on my command. You will free yourself from inhibitions and let your companions speak. Do you understand?"

"Yes, I understand," Kevin answered tonelessly.

"Good. You will open your eyes when I snap my fingers, but you will remain in a trance. Do you understand?"

"Yes."

Nicholas snapped his fingers. Kevin opened his eyes and stared straight ahead, purposely trying to make his face limp and expressionless.

"I do not want to talk to you, Kevin," Nicholas said. "I wish to speak to those within you."

Kevin flickered his eyelids and twisted his face, mimicking what he thought Nicholas looked like when he did it.

"Who are you residing in the body of this man?" Nicholas demanded.

Making his voice sound deeper, Kevin said, "I am known as Magnus."

"Where are you from?"

"I was a high priest in Atlantis, the leader of many souls. I have inhabited this body to bring my message to the faithful."

Nicholas leaned back in his chair and rubbed his chin thoughtfully. "You will come forth and speak when I call upon you?"

"I have waited many years for an opportunity such as this. It is only now that I have found a channel suitable enough to transport me to your dimension."

"Your time has come. I will call upon you to speak before my congregation. You can reach many people in this manner."

Kevin twisted his face into a crooked smile, struggling to keep his real laughter from coming forth. "A wise decision."

*   *   *

Nicholas stood before the congregation beaming. He looked royal and dapper in his charcoal gray suit. Kevin wore the sky blue silk robe.

"Brothers and sisters," Nicholas said, clenching both fists in front of him. "Tonight I give you Brother Kevin, a new channel for the word of the Lord." He held out his hand. The crowd applauded. Kevin smiled

46

sheepishly, then stood and bowed, feeling silly wearing the robe.

"He is the channel for an advanced spirit, once a high priest in Atlantis known as Magnus." Nicholas turned to face Kevin. "Are you ready?"

Kevin nodded.

Nicholas turned his back to the crowd, held his hand close to Kevin's face and snapped his fingers. Kevin's head dropped to his chest.

"Brother Magnus," Nicholas said dramatically, "High priest of Atlantis, come forth and enlighten the multitude."

A low growl came from Kevin's throat. His head rose. He opened his eyes and forced his voice, trying to make it sound otherworldly. Now he'd really shake things up.

"Magnus is not here. I am his mentor."

The room fell silent.

"And who might you be?" Nicholas asked, a puzzled expression filling his face.

"I am known among spirits as Malachi."

"Where are you from?"

Kevin worked his mouth from side to side, drawing the moment out before speaking. "Everywhere and nowhere. I am a multidimensional personality, inhabiting many planes simultaneously. It takes a great deal of energy for me to manifest through this mortal. That is why I sound as I do. Tonight, as you would call it in earthly terms, the alignment of forces is precise."

"Praise the Lord!" Nicholas cried.

*   *   *

Kevin grew more comfortable with his new role as the weeks passed. At each service Nicholas circulated among the congregation, inquiring about the lives of his followers while Kevin stayed in the background listening to what they discussed, using the personal elements he overheard to liven up his Malachi speeches. Each time he came up with new surprises and insights.

Nicholas acted as the master who could call forth advanced spirits and Kevin played his part as the channel, at first reciting routines Nicholas had performed, then coming up with more and more of his own original speeches. The congregation grew every week until their numbers quadrupled.

*   *   *

"We have to move to a new location," Nicholas said one night. He put his hand on Kevin's shoulder and squeezed, making Kevin flinch. Kevin looked at Nicholas. No question about it. He had his "channeling" act down pat and knew how to play the crowd.

"You're doing great, Kevin. Do you realize how much good you've done for these people?" His eyes took on the faraway look that Kevin had come to expect whenever Nicholas got sappy with his advanced spirit crap. These people were a bunch of sheep and regardless of what Nicholas said, he was playing them for suckers.

"I'm not doing anything," Kevin said, checking again like he always did to see if Nicholas still believed his act. "I'm nothing. It's Malachi who is the great one. I only allow him to come through."

"But that is the wonder of it." Nicholas rose and paced back and forth. "Your selflessness makes you one with the universe. It takes a great soul to sacrifice your own ego so others can reap the benefit of the wisdom that pours through you."

If Nicholas didn't believe, he was one hell of an actor himself, Kevin thought. He looked the older man deep in the eyes and saw only sincerity. No way could this guy be acting. He believed with all his heart.

Just like the rest of them.

*   *   *

"We'll be moving in a less than a month," Nicholas said one night as he and Kevin finished dinner. "I've found an old church building. We'll start remodeling in a couple of days." Nicholas's thick lips parted in a wide grin, showing his big teeth. "I'm bringing in a video crew for our first gathering. We'll make Malachi tapes and sell them at the door and at the new age bookstores. I plan on sending copies to television stations..."

"Television? Me?"

"Not you. Malachi."

Oh, Jesus, Kevin thought. What if my mother sees me dressed in this silly robe on T.V.? "Did you ever think about asking me if I want to be on television?"

Nicholas let out an exasperated sigh. "I don't mean this the wrong way, but no one cares about you. It's Malachi they want to see. People can't pay enough to hear him speak. They don't fit in this place anymore. It'll only be a matter of time before they fill up the new church."

"They don't care about me? It's me they're coming to see! You're the one they don't care about."

Nicholas chuckled. "You're right. They don't care about me either. They care about how I make them feel. They care about me caring for them." He held his hands close to his chest. I am the way and Malachi is the light."

He thinks I'm nothing, Kevin thought. He doesn't have a clue. I am Malachi. If I didn't do his little mumbo-jumbo dance, he would still be doing his one man street act. I'm the one that made things happen. *Me*.

He looked at Nicholas and saw the same far away, goofy look and knew that arguing would be futile. Nicholas had his mind made up and no matter what Kevin said, Nicholas wouldn't hear. He'd go off on one of his tired babblings about doing the right thing and bringing the light and enlightenment into people's lives. Kevin couldn't stomach another one of his gushing speeches. "I'm not so sure about this." He rose abruptly from the table. "I need to think it over."

"There's nothing to think about," he heard Nicholas saying from behind him as he stormed out of the kitchen. "The decision's already been made."

"We'll see about that."

*   *   *

After their last meeting at the old storefront, Kevin decided to make his stand. "I don't need you anymore," he blurted. "The congregation follows *me*, not you."

"What do you mean, you don't need me? If it wasn't for me, you'd be a nobody."

Kevin crossed his arms. "I can go into a trance by myself, without your help."

A hurt expression filled Nicholas's face and his eyes filled with tears. "But I've worked hard to get you where you are."

"And now you're holding me back."

Nicholas stood, fists clenched, lower lip trembling. "You can't do this!"

"Oh yes I can. *I'm* in control here."

Nicholas's mouth dropped and an uncomfortable moment passed between them before he spoke again. "Suit yourself," was all he said before stomping out of the room.

That was too easy, Kevin thought. I expected a lot more resistance, then again he's only a weak-minded holy roller. Without a backbone.

*   *   *

Kevin called for a special gathering of his followers in a new place. Without Nicholas. To his delight the congregation followed him, not Nicholas. Pleased with the turnout, Kevin surveyed the hall. *They know who has the power.* He took a seat up on the platform, closed his eyes, took a deep breath and paused dramatically.

Silence hung over the room like a thick, new fallen snow, yet the atmosphere felt charged with expectation. Kevin slouched back in his chair on center stage, immobile. The audience waited.

A moment later he jerked and became animated. His mouth moved. His hands gestured, but the movements weren't his. Something else manipulated him like a puppet. He struggled to regain control of himself, but the harder he tried, the more control he lost.

What's happening? He thought. His body grew colder. I've never felt like this before. He made an effort to focus his thoughts, but they scattered like trash in the wind.

He strained again with all his will, then gave in to unfathomable loss and hopelessness. Warmth spread across his lap and urine ran down his leg. His breathing came deep and labored and his features twisted into a painful grimace that made his face feel as if it were caving in. His eyes blinked before narrowing into an exaggerated squint. He peered intently as if lost in deep thought and a great pressure bore down on him making his head sink lower into his shoulders.

His body jerked again as though jolted by some great electrical current, and he came to life, but this life belonged to something infinitely darker and frightening than anything he had ever conceived of. Its force came through as a presence that focused itself in reverberating tones that spoke through Kevin, forcing what remained of his personality down into a tiny, cramped corner of his mind.

"I sit at the right hand of the Lord," a distant, alien voice said. "I was there at the beginning, and shall be at the end. I have witnessed the birth and death of many civilizations. Many worlds. None who have spoken to you in the past can match my might and power. I claim possession of this mortal in the name of sweet Lord and Master."

"Praise the Lord," Nicholas cried from the back of the hall.

"Praise the Lord," the audience answered in unison.

DRESSED TO KILL

The old man sure is dressed to kill today, Dan thought as he studied his father. Charcoal pinstriped suit, starched white shirt and his favorite red silk "power tie". What was left of his hair lay neatly combed, the part perfect. His gold signet ring glittered on his right hand. His "lure."

He said that people saw it as a sign of wealth and status that made them yearn for a piece of his success and want to do business with him. "Clothes make the man," Dad said. "If a man wants to be somebody, he's got to dress for success."

Dress for excess, Dan thought.

He felt his old anger rekindling, starting the all-too-familiar boiling in his stomach, so he stuck his trembling hands into his pockets and turned from the casket. The old man was dressed to kill, all right. Too bad he was already dead.

Dan looked over at the shell of his mom sitting in the corner with Phil Williams, the family lawyer. She looked thin and frail, as if the next strong breeze would whisk her away, another victim of the iron will of Daniel Trevor Lewiston The Fourth.

Not me, Dan thought. Bastard tried, had to give him that. Tried to take control of my life the same way he dominated mom's.

"What do you mean, art school?" he'd asked, less than two days ago. "First you want to be a worthless musician, and now this? You don't have an aptitude for either one." He leaned back in his leather chair, took a pull on his cigar and shook his head.

Dan sat on the other side of the mahogany desk in the study, the smell of old books and cigars suffocating him the way his father's stubbornness had strangled his dream of being a songwriter. He hated this room and everything it stood for. Hated his father and all his trappings. Always had, ever since the first time his father "called him on the carpet" at the age of four to humiliate him for wetting the bed.

It wasn't that the old man had actually abused him. On the contrary, in the eyes of others, the old man spoiled him with an abundance of possessions. He never wanted for anything. No cruelty; at least not physically and not in public. The cruelties were mental, saved for private moments.

Dan had not lacked for anything -- except love. In his father's mind, love translated into one thing, love of money. He demonstrated this to his son with material possessions that little Danny soon lost interest in, but let young Daniel ask him for attention, or play catch, or go for a walk like the other kids did, and the old man brushed him aside.

"There you go again," the old man said, jerking him back to the moment. "Drifting off into never-never land. No wonder you turned out to be such a loser. Look at you. You dress like a slob. No tie. You need a haircut. Should've known you'd come here begging for a handout."

"A loan, Dad, not a handout. I'll pay it back in a couple of months…"

"You're dreaming, son. It'll be another waste of money, nothing more. Come to work at the firm…"

"Dammit, Dad, for once can you let me do what I want!"

Dan recalled what he thought of as a string of bad luck that followed him through his endeavors since the first time he rejected his father's offer of a job with "the firm". He suspected that his failures were due to something more than bad luck. Maybe his father's influence had once again slithered into his life, the same way it had in school. "It's been you, hasn't it? You're the one who's been ruining things for me."

"No, it hasn't been me." His father's voice rose and his nostrils flared. "If there's one area you don't need help in, it's this one. You've screwed things up all by yourself."

The old man softened his tone. "I honestly don't understand what's wrong with you," he said, shaking his head. "Why can't you take some initiative like I did? No one helped me."

"Bullshit. You wouldn't have been a success at all if it hadn't been for your partner."

Daniel senior's head jerked back as if he'd been slapped. His face flushed and his mouth tightened.

Dan savored the moment; the first time he had ever seen his father speechless. He thought of his father's previous two heart attacks and the doctor's warning. The thought of having power over the old bastard filled him with savage glee.

The old man started to shake. His complexion passed from pink to crimson. "You ungrateful little bastard! You'll never amount to anything..."

Dan realized how much he hated his father. If the old man croaked, his problems would be over. The money would be his. "Hey, dad, you know what?"

He would never forget that puzzled expression. "Fuck you!"

His father half rose out of his chair. "You little shit -t - t," he stuttered. Spittle flew, clinging to his lower lip and dribbling down his chin onto his power tie. The color on his face nearly matched his tie. He grabbed at his chest and fell forward, twitching on his desk, the heart attack ending his life.

Seems like ages ago, Dan thought. He walked toward the rear of the funeral parlor, feeling his mother's accusing stare burning into him. He looked up and she turned away, burying her face in a handkerchief. Dan shook his head and stared down at the floor. When he reached the back of the room his gaze met the hollow eyes of his dad's lawyer.

Williams leaned over and whispered something to his mom, then rose from his chair.

Here it comes, Dan thought, steeling himself. The old lawyer shambled toward him, stooped like a walking corpse. His skin looked dry and colorless on his spindly frame as if all the juice had been sucked from him long ago. Dear old dad had a way of squeezing the life out of anyone who came under his influence.

Williams nodded and cleared his throat. "My condolences."

Dan didn't answer.

"I know this seems like an inappropriate time, but it is my duty to request your presence for the reading of the will."

"When?"

"When is it convenient for you?"

"Eight o'clock tonight."

"He's not even buried yet."

"He is as far as I'm concerned."

*   *   *

53

The three of them sat in the study, Dan to one side, chain-smoking, his mother across from him, head bowed. Dan could never remember her holding her head up. Behind the desk, in his father's seat, Williams shuffled through papers, spreading them across the desktop. When he seemed content with their arrangement, he cleared his throat. Dan sat up straight and glanced at his mother. Head still bowed, she looked sideways at Williams, like a child who did something wrong. Dan looked back to the lawyer who nodded, then began reading.

"I Daniel Trevor Lewiston The Fourth, being of sound mind and body declare this as my last will and testament. As has been my habit in business matters, I will be succinct. To my dutiful wife Elizabeth I leave the house, all my worldly possessions and all of my investments and interests, with the exception of my wardrobe."

Dan gasped, feeling as if he had been punched in the stomach. He looked at his mother. She put her head in her hands. Her shoulders shook.

"She may handle things as she sees fit, provided that she lets none of it fall into the hands of my worthless namesake."

Another punch.

The feeling in Dan's stomach shifted from icy hollowness to the familiar boiling rage that accompanied all of his dealings with his father. Even from the other side of death, the old serpent had put a chokehold on him. He glared at Williams who appeared to sink deeper into his chair.

"To my worthless son I leave my entire wardrobe so he can learn to be a successful man on his own. Clothes make the man. With this gift he can dress for success and make something of himself."

Trying to control me with his clothes! Dan thought. Like he did with everyone. With his goddamned clothes! He jammed his cigarette into the ashtray, sending up a flurry of sparks, then stormed out of the room leaving his mother behind, sobbing.

Anger raging, Dan stopped at the first bar he came to and ordered a double scotch and water. He downed it and ordered another. The bartender gave him a sideways glance with the third, but when Dan glared at him, he shrugged and said nothing.

God damn that cold-blooded old reptile, Dan thought as the numbness of the scotch took effect. He thought of his relationship with his father, playing back scenes from his childhood. Why couldn't things have been different? His anger dissipated into sadness, not because he had lost his father, but because he never had one. His family history was nothing more than a power struggle that dad always won.

Even after he died, he was still trying to win. Dan drained his drink and rose from the barstool. His head spun. He held onto the bar to steady himself, then drove back to his apartment, stopping first at a liquor store.

He stayed drunk the next day, nursing himself through the funeral with a hidden flask. He barely remembered the reception. When it ended, he managed to drive himself home, stagger up the stairs and fumble for his keys, gasping when he opened the door to find his living room stacked full of huge boxes.

He saw an envelope taped to the corner of the one nearest him. He tore it off and unfolded a short note written on his father's letterhead:

In spite of what you think, you are wrong to blame your father for your misfortunes. Your failures are entirely of your own making. He only tried to help. This delivery is his wish. You know how important it was for him to be prompt in his business matters.

Regards,

Philip C. Williams -- Attorney At Law

"My father's wish. My father's wish. Fuck my father! What about *my* wishes?" He ripped the note in half and kicked one of the boxes. "What about *my* wishes, you self-centered old prick?" He kicked again. "What about my wishes?" he screamed, launching himself at the pile of boxes, punching and kicking holes through them until he fell to the floor, sobbing and exhausted.

Dented and battered boxes lay strewn about. An arm from a suit hung out of one hole as if trying to escape, part of a shoe poked through another. He saw a mass of ties through a third. Breathing raggedly, Dan fought to calm himself. Other than his heavy breathing and an occasional sob, the room seemed silent.

Or was it?

He listened carefully and thought he heard a rustling sound, as if a small animal -- no, several small animals -- scurrying around inside the boxes. He sat up and tried to pinpoint the source of the noise. It seemed to be coming from more than one place.

"What the hell? Rats? Jesus Christ, did they send me a rat's nest?" He threw a haphazard kick at the box nearest him.

The strike agitated whatever was inside, which set off the boxes around it, the excitement jumping from box to box rising into a cacophony. Dan bit his knuckle, dragged himself to his feet and staggered backward away from the quivering boxes.

A moment later the arm of the suit sticking out of the box flopped about. The tear around it grew, then the shoe came to life, kicking angrily against its box, punching its way through. The tangled mass of ties rose from their hole, swaying to and fro like hungry moray eels.

Dan opened his mouth in a strangled scream and the clothes broke free and attacked. Shirts and pants flew through the air. Ties wriggled toward him. He turned to run, but a belt tripped him, then the suit coat flew over his head and a shoe kicked him in the gut, knocking the wind out of him. He tumbled to the floor, gasping for breath and wrestling with the suit coat. Something slithered up under his shirt.

He pulled the coat away from his face in time to see a red silk tie weaving between the buttons on his shirt, popping them in the process. The sensation of cool silk sliding over his skin sickened him. The tie coiled on his chest like a snake, its wide end hovering in front of his face like a cobra poised to strike. He tried to scream again and the tie lunged toward his mouth.

His father's voice came from the darkness, and Dan smelled his cigar, there in the room with him. "Clothes make the man," the voice said. Dan realized that it had to be a bad dream. His father was dead.

"They made me," his father's voice continued. "Now they're going to make you. I tried my damnedest to make you follow my path, but all it got me was a heart attack. Now you'll have to follow in my footsteps whether you like it or not."

Dan felt pressure on his throat. He shook his head from side to side to rouse himself from the nightmare.

Taking a deep breath, he sat up and rubbed his eyes. His feet felt strange, as if his shoes were too tight. He pulled his hands away from his face and looked down at his feet. His breath caught in his throat.

His father's shoes!

He scrambled up off the floor, switched on the light and stared wide-eyed at his reflection in the mirror. He looked impeccable, dressed in his father's favorite suit. Dazed, he reached up, absently touching the tie, and felt it tightening around his neck.

SLEEP, PERCHANCE DREAM

A full moon rose over the mountains, sending shafts of silver through the forest. Denver Martin sat up and finger combed his hair, stopping when he felt something sticky at the back of his head. He drew his hand back and saw dark fluid. Touching a fingertip to his tongue, he tasted blood.

Fighting panic, he tried to stand. Pain shot through his right leg, making him fall backward. Reaching down, his fingers brushed a warm gaping wound. Hot needles of pain shot through his hip, coalescing in a flash that left him in darkness.

Coming to in his room, Denver touched the back of his head, jerking his hand back when it brushed a tender spot.

He swung his legs over the side of the bed and the pain in his leg hit, dull and throbbing like an old ache. He pulled down his pajama bottoms, amazed to see a fresh scar across the girth of his leg.

*　　　　*　　　　*

Two hours later Denver sat in Dr. Lowenstein's office at the Lucid Sleep Study Center, looking up at the degrees and certificates that covered two of the paneled walls. Leather bound volumes filled another. A large flat screen monitor sat to one side on his desk.

The office door opened and Lowenstein hobbled into the room.

"You had another hyper-lucid dream?" he said, after settling into his chair. "And you have an injury that has stayed with you when you awoke?"

"That's what I said."

Denver rose, unbuckled his belt, and let his pants drop, pointing to his scar.

Lowenstein leaned forward, studying the wound. "Tell me about these dreams."

"He's always there. I can't see his face, but I feel his presence."

Lowenstein leaned back and folded his hands on his chest.

"He keeps pushing me more and more. Sometimes he chases me. Sometimes we meet head on. I tried making him leave, but the harder I push, the harder he pushes back." He straightened his leg and winced. "Until this."

"I need to look at your EKG's, REM, and FMRI files, along with your physiology records to see if I can detect any patterns," Lowenstein said, nodding toward his flat screen. "If this is too much you can always drop out of the program…"

"No way," Denver said.

*　　　　　*　　　　　*

Denver lay on his back staring through the pine trees. A branch cracked off in the woods, followed by a rustle in the brush. Panic sang through him when he heard laughter and the woods came alive with sound, then the laugh receded.

"Come back here, you son-of-a-bitch."

The laugh echoed back louder.

"Chickenshit!" Denver yelled, stumbling after the voice. "If I ever get my hands on you, I'll…"

"You got your hands on me last time," it answered.

*　　　　　*　　　　　*

"I ran into him again last night," Denver said, dropping into the chair across from Lowenstein in his office.

Lowenstein looked up from the waveforms and graphics he'd been studying on his monitor.

"I *know* his voice, but I can't place it." Denver held his thumb and forefinger apart. "I was this close to seeing him."

"I want you to stay in the Dream Lab for a few days," Lowenstein said quietly. "I think we're on the verge of a major breakthrough. Come and go as you please, but I want you to sleep there at night with full telemetry so I can observe you. If I can wake you in the middle of one of these episodes, I think we can solve this puzzle."

*　　　　　*　　　　　*

A few nights later, Denver drifted off to sleep in a bed in the LSSC Dream Lab with a cluster of tiny wires attached to his scalp and a custom FMRI imaging cowl over his head. Sensor wires snaked down his neck into a cable taped to the side of his bed, which connected to a console with two monitors on each side. Lowenstein and an undergraduate huddled over the console.

"He's in level one R.E.M. now," Lowenstein said. "I don't expect any activity until he's close to the end of his fifth cycle."

The undergrad scanned the console, then sat back in a chair with a magazine. "Why don't you take a break, Doc? I'll rattle you if anything happens."

Denver looked up at the moon bathing the mountainside in a pale silver glow. His adrenaline surged.

The undergrad watched the monitors to Denver's left blossom to life with waveforms and images. "Normal alpha and beta cycling," he said aloud, checking the other readouts.

Denver couldn't see the man's face when he came over the top of the hill. He took a deep breath and stood. "I knew you'd come." He clenched his fists. "You've been trying to drive me over the edge."

The right channel became active, bringing another response from the left, as if the two sides of Denver's brain were having a dialogue.

Denver knocked his tormentor to the ground, grappling and clawing until they stopped at the base of a boulder. Scrambling to his feet, Denver backed away from his attacker. Blood from a gash in his forehead ran into his eye. He squinted in the pale light, then the man barreled into him, catching him in his mid-section. Grabbing his attacker's waist, Denver fell back on the dirt flipping his opponent over his head.

"Dr. Lowenstein," the undergrad called out. "You'd better come see this."

Each display took turns jumping in succession, before their waveforms flatlined. Denver stopped breathing.

Denver and his adversary locked hands tight on each other's throats. Denver's mind darkened. He squeezed tighter and his opponent's grip loosened.

Panicking, the undergrad ran to Lowenstein's office, stopping when he saw the skin on Lowenstein's neck dimpling inward. A strangled gasp escaped Lowenstein's lips. His face flushed crimson. Finger-shaped bruises appeared on his throat before his body went slack. The undergrad tried to resuscitate him, but his efforts failed.

Lowenstein asphyxiated.

ON A WING AND A PRAYER

Agent Bennett pulled the Border Patrol cruiser down a dirt road in the middle of a field somewhere east of San Ysidro, stopping behind a stand of Eucalyptus. "There." He pointed through the trees and handed me his binoculars.

The house looked like a poor man's version of Hearst Castle. Rows of weathered, wooden frame wire bird cages faced it on three sides, joined at right angles, enclosing a giant U-shaped yard with the ramshackle house at its center. The years had bleached its wood shingles silver-gray. A blackened fire ring sat in the open area between the house and the cages.

Birds are living better than the humans, I thought.

"Seven dead," Bennett said. I glanced over to see him smile as he studied me with a lifeless stare; as if his eyes and mouth were two different people. Every time he opened his mouth I liked him less. Six years with the Border Patrol had made him into a bitter, cocky smart-mouthed punk. I didn't know how much more of him I could take. Two days was already too long.

Since there were deaths involved, the powers that be ordered a joint investigation between Homeland Security and The FBI. I was assigned to the case out of the San Diego FBI office and I got stuck with Bennett.

"Cancer patients," I said. "People with terminal conditions that killed them on installment plans. People who didn't want their savings drained in a hopeless battle when they could check out and leave their families taken care of."

"Fucking murderer," Bennett said as if I hadn't spoken.

"You're going to have a hell of a time making it stick. Every one we

61

talked to in a thirty mile radius had someone in their family or a friend healed by him. He's practically worshipped by most of them."

"He's a wetback Kevorkian," Bennett shot back. "Poisons 'em with plants. Uses that Devil's weed. Datura."

"You won't find anyone to testify against him."

Bennett gave me a smug grin. "You'll see when it gets dark around here and they start their who doo voodoo chicken dance and all that other crazy shit, 'cept in Alejandro's case, he's too cheap to buy chickens. He does a pigeon dance."

"Why wait?" I said. "We have the warrant. You know he's in there. Let's go talk to him now. Get this shit over with."

Bennett shook his head. "I want to catch him in the act, then drag his taco-bending ass away in handcuffs in front of all the other beaners. Make an example."

I couldn't believe what I was hearing. If you looked up "asshole" in the dictionary, they'd have Bennett's picture. Worse thing was, I had to go along with him. This was his show.

I looked through the binoculars again, trying to shut him out. A man came out of the house. Barrel chested, with big arms. Looked like a dark-haired bull with a thick mustache. He wore an old fedora with a white feather sticking up from its brim, making him look like some wild west Indian.

"Someone's coming out," I said.

"Let me see."

I handed Bennett the binoculars. He looked through them for a minute before giving them back. "That's Alejandro. Probably coming out to fly his birds."

"Fly his birds?"

"Watch."

Alejandro went to the end cage of one of the rows, opened the door, thrust his hands in and came out a moment later with a pair of white birds, which he tossed into the air. Moving down the row, he loosed two birds from each cage, looking up and smiling as each pair took wing. They flew high, coming together as if some giant invisible hand had taken them into its grasp, then they moved as one, back and forth, over and around, spinning, twisting, and turning; one perfect "V" dancing in the sky with the grace of a conductor's hand.

All the while Alejandro looked up, joy filling his face. His right hand fluttered as though he were the conductor. His body swayed with the dance of the birds, lips moving in what looked like a song or a prayer. He held both hands out and tilted his body back as though embracing the sky.

The birds dove like a huge dark arrow, plummeting straight for him. My heart dropped with them until the last possible moment, when the dark arrow exploded in a flurry of white. The birds spread their wings, fluttering out in a snowstorm of feathers, floating to rest on Alejandro's arms and shoulders.

"Pretty wild, huh?"

Amazingly enough, Bennett had kept his mouth shut during the whole thing. "I've never seen anything like it."

"That's just his opening act," Bennett said. "Soon as it gets dark, the real show starts."

*   *   *

They started showing up around sunset; Mexicans in beat up pickups, old primered Chevys, and Cadillacs, all lining the dirt road, bringing baskets of fruit, boxes of vegetables, chickens, eggs, blankets, and other gifts. Bennett got busy with the radio calling in backup, promising me that most of the visitors would be illegals.

While the Mexicans converged on the fire ring, our own area swelled with uniforms, trucks, and firearms. I thought about Waco and Wounded Knee and felt butterflies in my stomach. I hoped to God it wouldn't turn out like that. These guys knew what they were doing, but I regretted not calling in a few of my own field agents for back up.

"Okay," Bennett said into a handset. "Let's move out quietly. I want everyone on the perimeter a hundred yards out. Surround the whole place. We'll sweep in from four sides so none of 'em slip through. Get in position and wait for my signal."

Since I would be the one taking final custody of the suspect, I went in the front with Bennett to witness the arrest, but I was under orders to let the Border Patrol make the collar and do the initial questioning. I thought it was stupid, but it was the bureau's way of showing cooperation, and the Border Patrol had been the ones who initiated the investigation.

We moved through the shadows along the driveway until we came even with the house. Crouching by its side, we watched Alejandro in the firelight, lit in a blaze of orange that gave life to a magnificent headdress and feathered robe. He looked like an Aztec God with folded wings of fire that burned in flames of red, blue, and green.

A young woman lay on a cot in front of him, hands at her sides. Alejandro leaned low, chanting in soft Spanish. He blew smoke from a pipe up and down the length of her body, then waved a bird wing over her, gently dispersing the smoke.

"Move in," Bennett said into his radio. He started toward the fire, pump shotgun at the ready. I pulled my .38 and fell into step behind him. Uniformed Border Patrol agents came from behind bushes, trees, and bird cages, all carrying shotguns like Bennett's.

Alejandro straightened and made calming gestures to the crowd, all the while keeping his gaze steady on Bennett. The other agents moved in, herding the people away from the fire while the surrounding fields came alive with the roar of truck engines and the beams of headlights. Bennett moved around behind the medicine man while another agent held a shotgun to the Mexican's chest. Alejandro remained expressionless.

While the Border Patrol herded the crowd into transport vehicles, Bennett went through a collection of vines, cactus, mushrooms, leaves, roots, berries, seeds, and feathers spread out on a blanket. Shaking his head, he reached into his pocket, making a show of patting down Alejandro and producing a baggie full of white powder. "Looks like he'll be up on more than murder charges," Bennett said, matter-of-factly. "Possession of narcotics. Smuggling. Harboring fugitives." He signaled another man who said something into a radio.

Five minutes later, a Border Patrol step van pulled up. Bennett unlocked the back doors and manhandled Alejandro into the windowless truck, motioning with his head for me to follow.

A wall of riveted metal separated the front seats from the rear of the van. A window, barely big enough to pass a hand through had been set in the center of the wall toward the top. Bennett pushed Alejandro into a corner and dropped into a bench beside him, pulling out a notebook. "If you want to cop to the murder beef, we might consider dropping the drug charges," he said, dangling the baggie of powder in front of his prisoner.

"I took no one's life," Alejandro said in a heavy Spanish accent. "They left their bodies behind by their own choice. I only guided their spirits to the other world."

"Yeah, you guided 'em all right," Bennett muttered. "You made up that Jimson Weed brew that killed them." He rose and motioned toward the door with his thumb. "Let's leave him alone for a while so he can come down off of whatever he's on."

"I want to talk to him," I said.

"You'll get a chance to talk to him back at HQ. Let's go."

"Hey, Bennett," I said, pissed that he had tried to order me. "You go. I'll come along when I damn well feel like it."

He gave me a menacing glare, which pissed me off even more. I stood and the fire disappeared from his eyes. He hurried out, quickly closing the door behind him.

I turned back and saw the trace of a smile on Alejandro's face. I couldn't help smiling myself, then we both chuckled. I forced myself to get back my composure. "I don't know what you did to get him so wound up," I said, "but he has it in for you. No matter what happens, he's going to do everything he can to make your life miserable."

"His anger is all he has," Alejandro said. "I feel great sadness for him."

"After what he's trying to do to you?"

"He can give my body discomfort, but he cannot hold my spirit. It flies with the birds." He made a sweeping gesture.

I couldn't help but admire his conviction. Here he was handcuffed, locked in a van, headed for deeper, more dangerous confinement, and he still thought himself free. I looked in his eyes for signs of intoxication, but truth be told I had never seen eyes so clear, and the whole time Bennett antagonized him, his expression remained passive. I couldn't have stayed that cool, that's for sure. "Fly with the birds?" is all I could think of to say.

"My allies help me carry the souls of the dead over to their world."

I held up my hand. "Be careful what you say. It can be used against you."

He held my gaze, giving me a "You and I both know that's bullshit" look.

He didn't strike me as a murderer, especially after listening to all the people we had interviewed. None of them would testify against him. That's why asshole Bennett planted the dope. How the hell had I ever gotten involved in this mess? Dope was DEA territory, but Bennett had planted it. I should be arresting him.

"Do not worry about me," Alejandro said as if reading my thoughts. "Bennett is blind. He cannot hold my spirit."

"But he has your ass," Bennett said, yanking the door open. "We're pulling out," he said to me. "You're riding up front with me."

I had a half a mind to tell him, "Fuck you!" Alejandro was better company than Bennett, but I wasn't about to let that prick get away with planting dope. Any bust goes down with my name tied to it's going down clean or it ain't happening. "Be there in a minute," I said.

"So did you kill them?" I turned back to Alejandro, watching for a reaction.

"My spirit and my allies flew with them and guided their souls to the other world." His face remained impassive.

"I'll try to help you," I said, getting up.

His eyes stayed locked on mine. Amusement flickering behind them, then a slow smile filled his face. "You are a good man, *amigo*. I am thankful for the spirit of your offer, but I do not need your help. He cannot hold me. My soul is free." He nodded. "I will keep the spirit of your gesture in my heart just as my spirit will stay with you when this night is over. Now you must go. Bennett waits. *Adios*."

"*Adios*." I held his gaze a few seconds longer, thinking it the gaze of a man who knows he is saying goodbye for the last time. He dropped his head and started speaking in low Spanish. I didn't understand the words, but I could tell by their rhythm that he was praying. I turned and went out the back of the truck. Bennett glared in at him for a moment before closing and locking the door.

"Someone else is driving our car back." He held up a set of keys. "As the arresting officers of record, you and I are taking this package back personally." He started toward the front of the truck.

I climbed in beside him. "I'm not so sure..."

"Just to show you there's no hard feelings, I'm giving you half the credit for the bust."

"I don't want..."

He started the van and put it into gear. "You're not listening. I'm going to make you a star." He motioned with his head. "We got us a serial killer back there."

I couldn't believe what I was hearing. I knew something about serial killers. I had been to school in Quantico and had learned first-hand from the experts. "Are you serious or delirious," I heard myself saying. "He doesn't even come close to fitting any serial killer profiles."

"He does now," Bennett said. "I've got a cousin works for channel eight and I got word out to some of my other contacts. There are news crews waiting for us back in San Diego." He looked over at me, smiling with his best shit eating grin. "Our joint operation is going to be on the eleven o'clock news."

Shit. Bennett might get his spotlight, but I wasn't letting anyone go down for his pathetic frame up. "You're not going to get anybody to testify against him. Those people all wanted to die because their lives had become unbearable. They died by their own hands. In their sleep. Peacefully."

"What are you talking about?" he said evenly. "You're the one bringing the charges against him. You're the FBI."

"No one's going to go against a dead relative's wishes," I said. "You want to try and prosecute him for the deaths, you go right ahead. I'm not going to stop you, but I'm not going to let you get away with that plant the dope trick, either. I don't want any part of it. This whole bust is dirty. Count me out."

"I don't get it," he said, genuinely perplexed. "TV crews will be there. This is your chance to get some credit. The brass sees it, it could mean a promotion."

"Your fifteen minutes of fame will be solo." I said, waiting for him to return my gaze so he could see that I was serious. His face reddened and the veins in his neck stood out. I waited for the eruption and I wasn't disappointed.

"Fuck you," he said putting emphasis on the 'fuck'. His face contorted, reminding me of a frustrated infant that couldn't get what it wanted. "I try to hook you up and you throw it back in my face."

"Fuck you too," I said keeping my gaze steady. "I only make clean busts."

It ended there. At least the thick headed son-of-a-bitch knew I meant business. We rode the rest of the way back to San Diego without speaking. I glanced over from time to time to see him staring straight ahead, as if I weren't there.

My stomach did a slow roll when I saw the tall directional antennas sticking up from behind the fence of the Chula Vista Border Patrol lot. Vans from four television stations spread in a semi-circle like wagons braced for an Indian attack. Cameramen hustled, mounting their mini-cams on their shoulders, signaling their engineers. Lady newscasters checked their makeup, while men straightened their ties and checked their suits.

As reporters hurried to his door with microphones extended, Bennett looked at me one more time, his expression questioning. I shook my head no and stepped out my door. Thankfully they converged on the driver's side. Poor Alejandro had no idea what was about to happen.

I walked away from the van as fast as I could, not wanting to be associated with Bennett's circus in any way, then I circled around the back of the crowd. I heard him first, then saw him, flanked by two shotgun toting officers, literally in the spotlight, milking the moment for all it was worth.

"After months of intensive investigation in conjunction with other federal and local agencies, we've apprehended a known criminal with at least eight murders to his credit, possible drug connections, smuggling, and a number of other crimes."

He strutted toward the rear of the van, cameras tracking, reporters moving with him. When he reached the back doors, his two guards positioned themselves on either side. He stuck a key in the lock and turned once more to face the cameras. "Please keep your distance," he said holding his hands up. "This man is dangerous." He turned the key and pulled the door open. The cameras swarmed in behind him, bright spotlights illuminating the inside of the van. Bennett and the news crews stopped as if they hit an invisible wall.

I moved closer, peering over the shoulders of the people in front of me until I could see inside the van. A single white feather fluttered down as if dropped from the roof, landing on top of a pair of handcuffs that sat in the spot where Alejandro had been.

FUSION

Suzanne adjusted the focus on her electron microscope and watched two sets of cells swim into focus. "Okay," she muttered. "Let's see if they're happy." She set the cell electromanipulator to deliver a quarter second .02 microvolt pulse at 400 hertz and hit the actuation switch, making the cells dance.

The phone rang before she could check her results. She snatched it up. "Hello."

"How's it going, gorgeous?"

Marcus. Pleasant warmth swept through her as she remembered their last night together before he left town to meet with investors.

"Still banging away," she said, thinking of how he had hit all her pleasure zones. "If I can isolate the regenerative salamander gene and fuse it to mouse cells, I can replicate it in humans."

"If we show them regrown mouse limbs they'll be beating our doors down," Marcus said.

The unit beeped, demanding her attention. "I have to check this last cycle. I think I'm getting close."

She switched the cell electromanipulator to its high voltage range, set the output to deliver a one second 500 volt pulse at one megahertz and hit the switch. The two cell sets drifted toward the center of the field, then stopped to key her observations into her laptop.

> Dipole activity from a one second, 500 volt, one megahertz pulse. Cells approach field concentration, then stop. Increased field strength could enhance attraction.

She set the instrument to its maximum setting; a 20 microsecond, 3 kilovolt pulse at one megahertz. The cells jumped toward the field center and aligned themselves into chains. "Close, but no cigar," she muttered.

She tried different voltages and varying pulse lengths. Each time the cells aligned, then drifted apart. "Come on," she said to the electrode setup. "You mean to tell me you'll get close, but you don't want to kiss?" She keyed more notes into her computer.

> Maximum three kilovolt setting produced pearl chains. No arcing. Stronger field strength could induce breakdown of cell membranes so adjacent pores can form channels allowing an exchange of cytoplasm, leading to a hybrid. The problem lies in the field strength, but the power needed exceeds the limitations of the instrument.

She had the mouse and salamander cells in the same media and they'd formed chains. How could she get more field strength?

She studied the electromanipulator. A Celltron 3000, the most powerful instrument on the market. After rummaging through her desk drawers for a screwdriver, she unplugged the unit and broke the silver label covering one of the screw holes, ignoring the warning.

WARRANTY VOID IF REMOVED.
REFER SERVICE TO A QUALIFIED CELLTRON
TECHNICIAN.

A technician wouldn't give her the field strength she needed. She removed the rest of the screws until she had the back panel off. A schematic had been glued to the inside. A prominent red label stated:

DANGER HIGH VOLTAGE

She noticed the taps of the transformer added up to a total of 3500 volts. What were the extra 500 volts for?

Suzanne made a few calculations, then cut one of the wires and reattached it to the last transformer tap. According to the diagram, now it would put out 3500 volts. After plugging it back in, she set the instrument for its maximum setting, a 20 microsecond, 3.49 kilovolt pulse. She looked up at the cells on her monitor, wiped her sweaty palms on her lab coat and hit the switch.

Nothing happened.

"Shit!" She slammed her palm down on the bench and heard a buzz followed by a loud snap, then a blinding flicker sent slivers of glass flying. A second flash came on the end of the first, its sizzling lance staggering her backward. White hot fire arced into her brain. Smaller bits of glass peppered her face.

Her hand flew to her right eye, clawing at the pain. She knocked the offending sliver free and stared at it glistening amidst a tiny spot of blood on the end of her finger. Smelling acrid smoke, she looked up through the blur and saw a thin black trail spewing from the instrument. She yanked the power cord from the wall. Clutching her damaged eye, she went in search of help.

*   *   *

The brightness from the doctor's orthoscope made Suzanne's eye water, but she felt safe in his care. Dr. Rajah was City Hospital's leading eye specialist.

"You don't know how lucky you are," the short balding man said with an Oxford accent. "It's superficial. Severed a few capillaries, but otherwise barely nicked the surface."

She blinked, feeling a scratching sensation beneath her eyelid. "My eye will be all right?"

"Expect some blurring for a few days, but it should heal quickly. Tilt your head back please."

He pulled her eyelid up and applied a few drops of something oily, then pressed a piece of gauze over her eye and taped it in place. "I'll remove the patch in a couple of days. Get these filled." He scribbled out a prescription. "Two drops three times a day after I remove the bandage. The pills will kill the pain and help you sleep. Go home and rest. Come back on Friday."

"But I have to work…"

He scowled, his bushy eyebrows V'ing in the middle of his forehead. "No work. Your eye has been traumatized, not to mention the shock to your system. Besides you're run down."

"But…"

"Give your eye some time to heal," he said as if she hadn't spoken. "You'll be back at it soon enough."

*   *   *

Following his advice, she went home, took her medication and slept through the night and part of the next day until a far-off ringing woke her. She drifted toward waking, absently rubbing at the nagging itch in her eye. Pain startled her fully awake.

She opened her one good eye, confused by the gauze covering the one that itched, then the previous day's events rushed into her mind. The phone rang again.

She grabbed it in the middle of the next ring. "Hello?"

"Hey, babe, it's Marcus. I just heard what happened. You all right?"

She glanced at the clock on her nightstand. She'd slept for fourteen hours. "Doctor said I was lucky. He ordered me to take a few days off."

"I should be back in a few days. You sure you're alright?"

"I'm fine."

"OK. I'm headed into an investor meeting. Call me if you need anything. Love you."

"You too." She put the receiver down and gently rubbed at the scabs on her face, aching to scratch her bandaged eye.

Her head thumped when she crawled out of bed. Each excruciating pulse ended with a dull throb beneath her bandage. Her stomach did a slow roll. She went to her dresser and stared at her face with her one good eye, her hand stroking countless scabs.

She wasn't going to work looking and feeling the way she did. Her eye itched to the point of burning. She fought the urge to scratch and took more pain killers. When they kicked in, she forced herself to drink some juice and fell back to sleep.

The next forty-eight hours were a blurry, confused cycle of sleeping, awakening to the itch, and taking more sedatives. Each time Suzanne awoke, the itch burned more. Her stomach felt queasy, making her vomit twice. Thinking that the drugs and lack of food sickened her, she stopped taking her medication.

As its effects lessened, she roamed the house trying to clear her thoughts. Fuzzy images flashed through her mind. Mud. Worms. Insects. A craving she couldn't fathom, drove her to the kitchen. Peering into the refrigerator, she spotted a package of raw hamburger. Its cold greasiness satisfied her craving.

She looked at herself in the bathroom mirror. Most of the scabs had gone. Smooth spots shone where the skin had healed. The itch in her bandaged eye still nagged.

No more. The patch was coming off. Her eye needed to breathe. She closed the door, and worked by the night light, tugging at the bandage, keeping her eye closed while pulling away the last of the gauze. The cool air hitting her eye felt good, but her eyelid felt as if someone had placed a rock on it.

She concentrated on relaxing her facial muscles, then let her injured eye drift open. Everything blurred. She forced her eye open wider. Still fuzzy. Closing it again, she opened her good one. The night light, sink and mirror came into sharp perspective. She opened her right eye again. Still blurred.

She reassured herself that it needed time to adjust. Opening it fully, she stared directly at the night light. It looked like a thick layer of gauze covered it.

She leaned closer to the mirror and reopened her good eye. A thick jellylike mass had formed over her injured eye. The skin surrounding it looked smooth and discolored. She thought the growth might be mucous, but it looked thick and clear. Beneath the surface her pupil looked like the glazed eye of a fish on ice at the market. The skin on the nape of her neck twitched, then she vomited.

*   *   *

"Aside from the itch, my stomach's been nauseous." The cold leather padding on the examination table chilled Suzanne through its thin paper covering. She looked up at Dr. Rajah's obscure outline through the film of her eye as he probed its edges. She could barely see the light reflecting off his bald head.

"The skin around it is smoother too," he said. "It's a good thing you called." He stepped back, crossed his arms and wrinkled his bushy eyebrows. "I'm going to remove it."

"I don't think..."

"I have a laser," he said, patting her arm. "A little numbing and a few strategically placed strokes should take care of it."

She let out a shaky sigh. "I'll do anything to be rid of it."

Five minutes after applying drops that deadened the itching, Dr. Rajah had Suzanne sitting straight in a chair, her head clamped. She saw a hazy red dot and sensed the doctor's movements around the edge of her eye, but felt no pain. After feeling a brief tugging, her vision cleared. A wave of relief filled her, then a rose colored tinge washed over her vision. The doctor dabbed gently at it, a surprised expression on his face. "Amazing!"

"What?"

"It must have been a secondary infection, but beneath the mass your eye has healed perfectly. I've never seen one mend this fast. I want to run a few more tests, just to be safe." He placed the gelatinous mass in a small container. "I'll call you with the results."

He put fresh gauze over her eye and taped it, then motioned for her to stand. She leaned forward and grabbed at her stomach. Butterflies.

"Stomach still bothering you?" he asked.

She nodded.

He jotted a prescription on his pad. "Dramamine. Take them for a week or so."

"Can I go back to work?"

"Maybe in a couple of days."

*   *   *   *   *

Two days later, the itch in her eye still nagged, but it had diminished to a small discomfort and the uneasiness in her stomach had dwindled to a tiny flutter.

Anxious to see if her vision retained its clarity, she went to the bathroom to remove the bandage.

To Suzanne's delight, other than a tiny red line surrounding her eye, it looked clear. She could go back to the lab and pick up the remnants of her experiment.

She expected to find the lab in the same disarray she left it in, but the mess had been cleaned up. A brand new Celltron sat in the place of the old along with a new electrode stand. Marcus. How sweet!

She threw herself into her research, poring over her notes, setting up the equipment and formulating an approach that didn't need such a high field strength. Maybe a different media, she thought, or adding a cross-polarized magnetic field.

Days passed as she worked through formulas and theories. Other than a craving for raw eggs and rare hamburger, she felt great. The redness around her eye disappeared and her vision stayed normal.

On the first day of her new fusion trials, she received a call from Dr. Rajah.

"The results of your tests have come in," he said with his Oxford accent. "I'm a bit puzzled."

She felt a sinking feeling in her stomach.

"Can you come in this afternoon around two o'clock?"

"Sure."

"Drink as much water as you can before you come. We want to run a sonogram."

*   *   *

She found a tall, lanky man whose nametag identified him as Dr. Jansen with Dr. Rajah. They had a sonogram unit wheeled into the room with two small monitors.

"There's no need to be upset," Jansen said, as if reading her mind. "We want to check out your internal organs and circulatory system."

He wheeled the sonogram unit next to the examining table so Suzanne could watch. She held her breath while he guided the probe around her breasts and neck. When it passed over her abdomen, a large mass came into view. He hit a few buttons to magnify the image. A long, curved body with a long tail and an elongated head swam into focus. Four tiny clawed feet scrabbled for purchase inside an egg-shaped sac.

A ROSE FOR EMORY

Emory and Chris watched old man Johnson shamble between the compost heap and the dilapidated greenhouse that occupied so much of his time. Overalls hung from his spindly body like rags on a scarecrow and his thick white hair stuck out at odd angles from his baseball cap. From their perch on the roof of the garage next door, his wrinkled face looked like a giant prune.

"He's a strange old bird," Emory said. "Heard lots of stories about him. They say he killed his wife by choking her."

"Choking her?"

"Word on the street is that he jammed a rosebud down her throat so he could get her insurance money, but the cops never proved he did it. Since she croaked, all he does is garden. Just roses."

"Can't tell from looking at that dump," Chris said. At fifteen, he was two years younger and a full head shorter than Emory. He had thick black hair, dark brown eyes and a pouting lower lip that made him seem on the verge of crying.

"He's always out there." Emory pushed a shock of red hair away from his dark eyes and took a hit from the joint Chris handed him. "Even at night. In and out. In and out. I think he's burying his insurance money out there."

He studied Chris with hooded eyes while his brain went to work. In the past his scheming had earned him free room and board in the county juvenile detention center. He thought of the money the old geezer probably had hidden in the greenhouse and smiled. "Smitty said he saw him dragging some bags out there."

Chris nodded and reached for the joint.

"Bet he keeps it in the greenhouse." Emory held the joint out to Chris. When the younger boy reached for it, Emory pulled back.

Chris squinted at the greenhouse. "I've seen his flashlight out there at all hours. He must be doing something."

"I guess we'll have to find out."

"You're not going to break in, are you?"

"No, stupid. *We* are."

*   *   *

That night, the two boys lay on the garage roof in silvery darkness. A flashlight bobbed eerily through the greenhouse like a gravedigger's lantern. After it made a circuit around the building, it disappeared into the house.

Emory and Chris slid down the drainpipe on the other side of the garage and crept around back waiting to make sure the old man wouldn't return, then they slipped through a hole in the fence and bolted for the moonlit greenhouse.

Emory gave one last look around when they reached the door, then grabbed the handle and pushed. The door creaked open and the two boys stepped into the moist darkness.

The thick scent of roses undercut by the damp smell of fresh earth filled their nostrils.

"God," Chris whispered. "Get a whiff of those flowers."

"Yeah," Emory said. "Reminds me of a funeral."

Row after row of neatly pruned rose bushes stood bathed in moonlight like sentries, poised for a command. Emory spotted a couple of spades standing in the corner. He elbowed Chris. "There's some shovels. Let's get digging. The money's got to be buried somewhere under the flowers."

They dug up bushes and tossed them randomly aside, becoming so engrossed in their work, neither heard the old man until he caught Chris in the beam of his flashlight.

"My roses!" he cried. "My roses!" The flashlight bobbed.

"You little shit! What are you doing to my roses?"

Chris froze.

Emory spun and let his spade fly in the direction of the flashlight.

A startled cry, then a muffled clang, and the shovel clattered to the ground. Emory's eyes widened and his mouth dropped. "What a shot," he whispered.

"Let's get out of here!" Chris shrieked.

Emory walked toward the old man, still disbelieving the accuracy of his throw.

Shit, he thought. I didn't think I'd hit him. Got him right on the noggin.

When he got to the door, he saw the old man's body sprawled in front of it, blood trickling from the corner of his mouth. A huge gash creased his forehead, a flap of skin exposing the bone underneath.

Emory gawked at the old man's glassy-eyed stare. The body remained still.

Chris rushed up behind, startling him out of his stupor.

"Is he? Is he?" Chris's hand flew to his mouth.

Emory squatted down and put his hand on the old man's neck, feeling for a pulse he knew wasn't there. "Dead," he said. His voice sounded hoarse. Raspy. His throat felt stuffed with cotton.

"Let's get out of here." Chris sounded as if he might burst into tears.

Coldness swept over Emory, filling him with icy resolve. "No," he said letting his confidence rise. "We can't leave him like this. Someone will find him, then we'll get busted. We have to hide him."

"Wh--where?"

Emory scanned the room until his gaze came to rest on the mound of dirt next to where he'd been digging. "There." He pointed. "We'll bury him there." He turned back. Even in the muted light of the greenhouse, he saw that Chris's face had lost its color. His hand remained at his mouth.

"Come on," Emory said. "Grab a leg. Help me drag him."

"I can't," Chris's voice quavered. "I can't touch him. He's dead."

"You don't grab him," Emory growled, "you'll be going in the hole with him."

Chris jerked. His eyes bulged. He shot Emory a sideways glance, then leaned over and grabbed one of the old man's legs. Together, he and Emory dragged the body toward the hole, dropped him next to it and dug deeper. They rolled the corpse into the hole, plopping it down face first in the dirt, and quickly shoveled dirt back in on top of him.

When the hole was almost full, Emory took the rosebushes they dug up and planted them neatly over the body, making the bed look uniform. He took off his shirt and wiped the handles of the shovels before putting them back, then he and Chris crept out of the greenhouse and went their separate ways.

"Catch you later," Emory said.

Chris didn't answer.

*   *   *

Emory awoke the following morning to the fragrance of roses. The scent caused him to sit straight up. After a moment's disorientation, he remembered the previous night and his throat went dry.

He threw back the covers and stepped out of bed. His feet touched something soft and feathery. Looking down, he saw rose petals scattered around his bed. A thin trail led to his window. He jerked his feet back and held them off the floor for a moment, then jumped out of bed.

Afraid his mother might find them, he cleaned the petals up and flushed them down the toilet.

He grabbed his cell phone to call Chris. It rang the moment his hand touched it, startling him.

"Emory, its Chris. I'm scared shitless. Something weird is happening. When I woke up this morning I found..."

"Rose petals around your bed."

A sharp intake of breath, finally a whisper. "How did you know?"

"Same thing here. Listen, keep your trap shut. Don't say nothing to nobody. Stay home and lay low."

A week passed with no further incidents. Chris and Emory slipped back into their old routine, staying clear of old man Johnson's place, neither of them talking about that night.

Exactly one week after the old man was killed, Emory awoke from a scratch on his cheek. He felt a stinging wetness and smelled roses. When he turned on the night lamp, he found a bloody thorn stuck through the pillowcase.

The same thing happened to Chris.

Another week passed. No one seemed to notice that old man Johnson was gone. Two weeks after the old man's death, Emory awoke to the smell of roses, this time stronger. He found no petals or thorns until he put on his slipper.

A large thorn pierced his toe.

He saw Chris limping at school. The two boys stared at each other from a distance. Neither spoke.

On the third week, Emory awoke before dawn, overpowered by the sickeningly sweet smell of roses. His hands and legs bled from scratches by thorns stuck into his sheets. Rose petals covered his bed, their red matching the blood staining the sheets.

He wiped sweat from his brow with a trembling hand, smearing blood on his palm. His head pounded. He climbed out of bed and washed himself off, then cleaned the mess from his bed and hid the sheets in his closet.

*   *   *

As a rose-colored sun peered over the horizon, Emory slipped out the back door and headed for old man Johnson's greenhouse.

The glass on the roof and sides glinted burnt orange. The plants inside cast wild shadows onto the glass wall. Emory paused, his eyes darting about, then he stepped through the side door.

The cloying scent of roses bore down on him, thick, moist, and heavy. The once neat rows of bushes grew out of control, crawling every which way.

Muted sunlight highlighted blood red blooms that darkened into deeper shades, the closer his gaze moved toward the old man's grave. Over it, the bushes grew exceptionally thick, like brambles. Hundreds of blooms blocked out the sunlight in that corner of the greenhouse. Emory felt drawn into the darkness.

He thought he saw a dim shape behind the thorn-studded copse and edged closer. His chest felt tight. Over the top of the growth, he saw Chris leaning against the wall, his head bowed toward his chest.

"Chris!" Emory stepped over some creepers and started toward his friend. "You asshole. You scared the shit..."

Streams of blood ran down the front of Chris's shirt. Emory stared dumbly at circles of thorn-spiked runners forming a grotesque collar wrapped tightly around Chris's neck. His lifeless face looked purplish-white and puffy. Bloodshot eyes bulged out of their sockets and his blackened tongue lolled out of his mouth. His throat was stuffed full of rose petals.

Something moved behind him.

Emory screamed. A sharp pain pricked his ankle as a growth snaked out from the old man's grave, trapping his foot. He pulled away, tearing a gash in his ankle. Tendrils of rosebuds slithered toward him, cutting off his escape. He leaped and dodged. Thorns bit into his legs and buttocks. Ten feet from the door branches leaped toward his back, slicing through his shirt into his skin, stinging him. Five feet from the door, spiked runners tripped him. More runners crept over him.

He thrashed, breaking some as others pulled tighter. Thorns shredded his clothes, sliced his arms, legs and chest. Blood covered his hands.

He pulled himself up into a sitting position. A heavy, musky scent of decomposing rose petals hit him in the face. Rotted overalls towered over him, then he saw the old man's face.

Sallow skin hung like dripping wax. One eye socket caked with dirt. A tiny sprout grew out of it. Two large earthworms slipped from one nostril, glistening like reddish-brown mucous. One eye stared straight at Emory. Beetles crawled over his head and arms. Maggots oozed from his cheeks.

Emory pulled back. Vines snapped. Flesh ripped, burned. Blood spurted. He lunged again toward the door and tumbled outside.

Emory slammed the door before old man Johnson's corpse reached it. He grabbed the wheelbarrow by the mulch pile and jammed it against the door. A bloody, pulpy fist smashed through the glass, fingers clenching and unclenching. Emory looked frantically around the yard and spotted a gas can. He prayed silently and dashed for it. Another hand punched through the glass. Emory grabbed the can, unscrewed the cap and doused the clutching hands, then he fumbled in his pocket for a lighter. When it flared to life, he touched it to one of the hands. It went up in a ball of flame. A strange sound, part gurgle, part moan, part scream, came from behind the door and the hands retreated.

Emory whipped open the door and threw more gas on the flaming corpse. It stumbled backward in a stagger-dance and fell into a row of rose bushes. Emory emptied the rest of the gas over the flowers and threw the can into the fire. Flames roared to life, backing him out the door.

Fire engines arrived a few minutes later, followed by the police. They picked Emory up three blocks away and took him to the hospital. Once his wounds were treated, the police questioned him, but he was incoherent so they brought him to the county mental health facility for observation.

Toward the end of his stay, Emory realized that no one would believe him, so he fabricated a story about Chris starting the fire and how he tried to stop him. The fire had roared out of control and Chris got caught in it. No evidence could be found to the contrary, so Emory was released.

After eating his first home-cooked meal in weeks, he went upstairs to bed. When he opened the door to his room, his breath caught.

A single red rose lay on his pillow.

DIMINISHING RETURNS

S cratch walked along, head down, trying to remember. He'd been Scratch for so long, he had forgotten his real name and the harder he tried to remember, the further it seemed to float out of reach, like grabbing at smoke. John? Pete? Charlie? Shit! Why couldn't he remember?

He shuffled down Broadway, not caring that he missed his dumpster stops. They didn't matter today. The name thing did. He felt as if his life depended on it. When was the last time anybody had called him by his real name?

His life had gone fuzzy. Everything. His mind. His body. His legs dragged like two wet bags of sand, and his eyes -- he wanted so bad to shut them; shut out the world and lose himself in the release that sleep brought, but he couldn't do that now. Not in daylight. If the punks didn't beat him or take the few measly possessions he had, the cops would make him miserable.

His thoughts drifted the way they did when he slipped off to sleep. Faces floated by; older people first, then younger ones, then guys his own age. All nameless.

A flurry erupted, reminding him of the cliché that your life flashed before you when you were dying. Places. Blue eyes. Lips. An eyebrow. An old house. Rice paddies. Guns. Uniforms. He looked down at his ragged field jacket.

They felt familiar, but he couldn't make any connections to times, places, or names. Couldn't remember who he was or where he had come from, but he knew -- where *was* he going?

Looking up, he saw mist and the fuzzy outlines of buildings. He blinked at the blur of passing cars. The sun looked weak and washed out. His footsteps sounded muffled like walking in deep snow. The sound of cars and the noise of the streets came to him as if he lived on the other side of a thick padded wall.

A tall man in a gray suit frowned at him and made a wide berth, eyes looking everywhere but at Scratch.

Looking down at the sidewalk, Scratch moved one step, then the next. Forward. Going nowhere. He saw patterns in the concrete that he hadn't noticed before. Kaleidoscopic forms that interlaced and connected into a larger snowflake that wove itself into an even larger one that continued on to still more.

He rubbed his eyes with balled fists. The patterns looked darker, and in their darkness more distinct, as if the blackness had substance. He saw that they tied into the sky too. Different sizes and patterns intertwined in an intricate web of snow flake doilies set off against a background of infinite black.

A gang of punks rounded the corner, coming toward him. Scratch braced himself for the inevitable abuse, but they walked past him without acknowledging his presence. Why had they ignored him? He stopped and looked down at his shoes. His hands. Fuzzy like everything else. He understood that he should be feeling fear, but instead he felt numb, empty, and without purpose; the same way he'd been feeling for as far back as he could remember.

And he was tired. So tired. It took all of his will to keep his feet moving. One step. The next. The giant snowflake web, or whatever it was, grew; each tiny kaleidoscopic pattern changing in unison with the larger whole. Scratch realized that the patterns weren't growing. Instead, the empty black behind them was emerging.

He stared at the sky, back at the ground, the buildings, the cars, the people, and saw that they too were part of the web that held and contained them. He studied his arms, then his hands and saw that yes, he too was part of the diminishing web.

Keeping his momentum, he accepted his fate and shuffled forward into the darkness without hesitation, fading as he'd been fading for as long as he could remember. Fading into nothingness until oblivion embraced him and he was no more.

No one noticed.

DESIGNER DRUGS

Rick Butler stretched his long legs in front of him and watched the drug dealers moving furtively through Central Park. Crank, crack, angel dust, smack, Ketamine, DMT, Ecstasy, LSD; he had done them all. Considered a "hard head" by anyone who knew him, Rick liked playing a dosage game of chicken with himself to see how much he could take. He liked it out there on the edge — and he never lost it.

The lines on his face told the story of his travels like the scrawling in an old sea captain's log. Rick weathered many a drug storm in his thirty five years. It showed in the depths of his ancient brown eyes and the strands of gray that streaked his dark hair.

Empowered by an inexhaustible trust fund, Rick considered himself a pioneer of inner space who pushed all the envelopes and enjoyed reality in as many different versions as he could get himself into, until he had been everywhere imaginable and unimaginable, then he became bored.

A dozen hits of blotter acid had become another unfulfilling experience; in spite of his attempts to study its effects. He longed for something to push him further past the borders of his experience.

In his quest for the ultimate trip he had first read about, then gone to South America where he drank Ayahuasca brews, inhaled snuffs, and drank nasty concoctions, half of which he couldn't remember. Sure, he had some pretty wild trips, but he also shit and puked his brains out — and he still hadn't found "the" experience.

In Brazil, he worked for weeks to get accepted into a sacred Indian ceremony from a shaman who supposedly had a secret plant mixture that the other *brujos* feared. After a stinking, sweaty canoe ride with a chicken-shit, skinny little wetback named Juan, he ended up on the dirt floor of a thatched hut with an ancient long-haired, Indian who painted himself blue from head to toe.

Two crimson five sided figures stood out on each cheek and a mass of colored feathers covered his head. He wore a necklace made of claws and teeth. Black and orange stripes streaked the man's chest. Rick leaned toward Juan and whispered. "He really believes this mumbo-jumbo shit, doesn't he?"

Juan drew back, his wide eyes betraying his fear. "This is no laughing matter, *amigo*."

The shaman uttered more jungle mumbo-jumbo.

"What's he saying?" Rick asked.

"You must respect the spirits of the plants before he can share their power with you. Though you cannot see them, their power is strong. They can take any shape they desire."

While Juan spoke, the shaman kept his eyes locked on Rick's as if his stare would bore the message into his brain.

"No sweat." Rick made a show of keeping his own stare zeroed in on the other man's. Silence hung between them before the shaman spoke again.

"There is one more thing," Juan translated.

"What's that?" Rick said, still staring.

"You must sacrifice a living creature to thank the allies for your vision," the guide said. "This must be done at the end of the ritual or the allies will come for their sacrifice and steal your soul."

"Okay, okay." Rick held up his hands. "I'll give them a sacrifice."

Juan's eyes darted from Rick to the shaman and back again. "I hope you are sincere. These people take their Gods very seriously…"

"I told you I'd do it," Rick said.

Juan said a few words to the shaman who remained motionless for a long moment before pulling a small leather pouch from his side and handing it to Rick. Rick took it and backed away. The old man's face remained expressionless.

When no one saw him, Rick slipped into the jungle. After making sure no one followed, he took off in the canoe, leaving Juan behind. He made it back to Rio de Janeiro where he spent two days tripping his brains out in a hotel room, then he flew back to the States, once again ending up back on his bench in Central Park, endlessly accosted by walking drugstores pitching their wares like carnival barkers.

"Crack, reefer, eight balls, bindles!"

Prostitutes, he thought. Selling dope just to stay high. He studied each one that passed, seeing the same lifelessness in their eyes until he became aware of the feeling of being watched. Whirling around, his gaze locked with that of another man whose eyes gleamed with a light all their own.

Charlie Manson eyes, he thought.

Small and wiry, the man had long, jet black hair, a goatee, and a single gold earring that stood out against tanned skin. He wore a battered army field jacket.

"Hi." He smiled with perfect teeth. "Name's Max. I've got what you're looking for."

Rick frowned. "How do you know what I'm looking for?"

Max winked.

"Even if you did know," Rick challenged, "what makes you so sure I'd buy it from you? What have you got to sell that's so different from the rest of these losers?"

"Designer drugs," the man said in a velvety, baritone.

"Oh, yeah?"

"That's right."

Rick studied Max's angular face until his gaze came to the earring; a gold pentacle with an inverted crucifix in the center. Something shifted in his mind.

"How much?" he asked.

*   *   *

The pills looked like blood red, transparent bits of plastic, but were small and pentacle shaped like Max's earring. Rick poked at them. Max said one would be enough.

He popped two into his mouth and headed for his girlfriend's apartment.

Rick had met Michelle in a college psych class a few years before. She shared his enthusiasm for drugs, but in a different manner. Her pleasure came from studying his reactions to them.

"Hey, babe," he said when she answered his knock. "Wanna try something new?" He held out the last hit.

"You know I don't do drugs."

"Yeah, I know. Just thought I'd ask."

She studied him with mahogany eyes, then pushed a curl of long auburn hair behind her ear and examined the pentacle. "Looks like windowpane."

Rick held the remaining hit between his fingers. "I don't think so."
He popped the last hit into his mouth and waited for over an hour, but
nothing happened.

"I'm pissed," he said, heading for the door. "I'm going to find that
guy and get my money back."

He felt an inward tremble that blossomed into a warm shiver. Chills
crept up the base of his spine and circled his head with an exquisite
tingling sensation, then colors exploded in his mind like the grand
finale of a fireworks display.

"Wow." He blinked, wide-eyed. "This *is* different."

Michelle grabbed her notebook. "Tell me about it."

He caught her movements out of the corner of his eye. Colored
lights trailed off her hands as she picked up a pen. Flecks of gold
danced in the brownness of her eyes, giving them an enchanting
brightness and depth.

"Colors. Magnificent -- and you. Your face, it's more beautiful than
any face I've ever seen."

She smiled, her teeth gleaming with shimmering silver sparks. Her
face and skin glowed with an otherworldly light. Rick couldn't take his
eyes from her.

Her smile faded. "Don't look at me like that. You're giving me the
creeps."

"Sorry, it's just that – that..." He stared down at his hands. They
glowed like Michelle's and his skin moved on the surface like a colony
of amoeba and protozoa flowing in their own dance of life. He looked
past them to the carpet. It too had a life of its own. Hordes of
indescribable multicolored alien insects marched across it, teeming and
undulating.

"What is it?" Michelle said, breaking in on his reverie. "What are you
seeing?"

"Life. Everywhere. Everything has life. Your face. My hands.
Millions of living creatures."

His perception shifted, heightening the intensity of his vision. The
fluttering, eerie light filling everything he looked at blazed brighter.
"Whoa, this is intense."

"What?"

He recognized Michelle's voice, but they sounded like they echoed
from the end of a long plastic tunnel. "Michelle?" His own voice
sounded distant. "Everything's brighter now." His face felt like
invisible hands molded it. He groped his way to the bathroom. "Have
to see what my face looks like."

The walls, the furniture, and everything else in the apartment lit up as though covered with colored phosphorus. If he stared at any one thing for more than a few seconds he saw tiny "things" crawling across the surface.

Like melting, incandescent wax, his face shifted and changed in the mirror until he looked brilliant and fancied himself a god-like being from a distant planet, then his features metamorphosed into a hideous, sub-human creature from a Saturday afternoon matinee -- then he saw the painted face of the blue shaman mocking him.

His hair twisted and writhed, each strand becoming its own single organism. His eyes spun in pinpoints of swirling light that drew him into their bottomless depths.

Beyond words.

He gasped and turned from the mirror. His surroundings grew brighter until the glare became painful. He held his hands up to block the light. They were brighter too, then the movement around him quickened into a more frenzied pace.

His stomach knotted.

"Too much." He grabbed at his hair, then vomited in a brilliant explosion of color.

"Rick?" Michelle's voice, barely audible now. "Rick? What's wrong? What are you doing?"

"I can't -- I wish -- I would -- I can't..." *find the words to describe.* He buried his face in his hands and felt it expanding.

Michelle spoke again, but her words sounded like a phone line cutting in and out. Rick only understood a few syllables through the din of his mind.

"Should...call? ... Do...help?"

Rick tried to answer, but his speech took on the same disconnected quality. He repeated his message over and over, only able to utter three words; "Out – of - control."

He never heard an answer, but both heard and felt his own scream when he took his hands away from his face.

His world had become even brighter.

The feeling of being swallowed jolted him. He had the sensation of sinking into the bathroom floor. Panicking, he forced his eyes open, but whether open or closed, it made no difference. The painful glow nearly blinded him. Every part of it came alive with frantic motion. He clawed and scrambled to pull himself out of the morass. Panting and sweating, he got on his hands and knees and pulled himself up on his feet, blinking in disbelief when he found himself back in the jungle.

My God. What's happening? I keep getting off -- getting off. It won't stop. My mind -- slipping.

A flurry of colored activity swirled at the other end of the room. *What the... What's that?*

A hideous egg-shaped apparition flew toward him, its tendrils rushing wildly about its head, its mouth wide, teeth bared in a gaping scream of unintelligible fury.

Going for my throat.

He staggered back and fell over, his arm flew out and his hand hit something long and heavy.

The beast attacked, fangs bared, its hot moist breath on his face. His hand wrapped itself around the heavy object. He swung hard, bringing it down on the beast's head again and again. It howled a mournful wail that faded into a smattering of words; "Rick... No..." It stopped, its breath no more than a gurgle followed by silence.

He stared at the green fluid gushing from it, covering his hands with stickiness, then he pushed the pulpy mass from on top of him and tried to stand.

Two more beasts ambushed him.

He struggled, but one of them pinned him while the other sank its needle-like teeth into his arm. Darkness came swiftly.

*   *   *

He opened his eyes to blazing colors and tried to sit up, but an unseen presence held him down. He strained to push himself up, but couldn't.

A rumbling off to his side made him turn his head to see a group of egg-things rush toward him again. Powerless to resist, he twisted, turned, and screamed, helpless to fight. He thought he understood part of their strange babble as the sting of one of their fangs burned into his shoulder.

"Been – like – this - days."

*   *   *

Trapped. Tubes of glowing fluids in and out of me. Arms pinned. Too tired to fight. Not important anymore.

Rick struggled to adjust to his new world. The colors and movement still came bright and lively. If he remained quiet, he could pick up snatches of conversation.

89

"Beat – girl - death."

*   *   *

He retreated deep inside himself, his only hope in repose. The colors stayed whether he opened his eyes or closed them; as strong and bright as the first day. He gave commands to his body but it refused to respond.

He felt vaguely aware of a stream of spittle running out of the corner of his mouth. He wanted so much to wipe it off, but couldn't. He could still hear snatches of his captor's voices.

"Strange – Dying – Hopeless."

CYBERLOVE

It begins as neurochemically charged inspiration bubbling up from the depths of Passion@lov.com, who waits impatiently as his system logs on. Will she be there? Pangs of longing leap through his heart like spawning fish, their energy tickling his soul until his body responds, seeking an outlet for his deepest yearnings.

He navigates through a series of menus until his email pops up. He closes his eyes while graphics fill his screen, envisioning each of the videos and digitized pictures she has sent him, playing them back in his mind like a slide show.

He wants so bad to connect.

Scanning his email, Passion@lov.com hovers in cyberspace, searching for a sign of his intended love, but the sight of her name does not grace his In Box. Realizing that there are no messages, and worse, no enclosures, Passion@lov.com's heart sinks and his emotions dim until he rereads her last message.

She will always be waiting.

Her words fan his desire, rekindling the elemental fire of his passion. His feelings for Desire@lov.com fill him, sending the power of his emotion charged thoughts dancing from his fingertips, into his keyboard. The energy of each keystroke transforms into charged silicon, making thoughts of his love for her form onscreen.

Passion@lov.com bears his heart and soul to the altar of his keyboard and monitor, making his love offering to the spirit of Eros that permeates cyberspace. When he has given his all, he hits the send button, broadcasting packets of passion that carry his feelings for her, fragmenting and scattering throughout the Internet like so many sperm homing their way to another point of love on the wire where he hopes Desire@lov.com is logged on.

His digitized emotions give his impassioned message the power to find passage through switches, routers, hubs, LANs, WANs, and satellites until it makes its way to a far off wireless network card where it leaves the hardware layer and embraces CPU processor cycles that allow his words and images to reassemble and be transmitted to a distant video screen that shoots electron charged emotion from its blazing pixels like cupid's arrows.

Passion@lov.com's yearning leaps off the surface, passing through the nerves of his true love's eyes, downloading and processing within the electrochemical circuitry of her brain until its passionate energy makes its way to its home in her heart.

ANIMAL MAGNETISM

Greg Friedman stumbled through rotting undergrowth somewhere in the Amazon, delirious with malaria. Vines tripped him, low branches tore at his skin, and his teeth chattered from the chills that wracked his fever soaked body. His world spun and the thick growth of leaves above him did a mad, swirling dance before darkness swallowed him.

He drifted up through chants and singing, recognizing some of it, but most of it sounded unintelligible. His body felt moist, yet cool and soothed. He opened his eyes and magnificent colors flashed in front of him. His vision sharpened and the brilliant feathered headdress and painted face of a shaman swam into focus.

Wet leaves and small plants covered his torso. A pleasant, spicy, cinnamon smell filled the air. His fever still burned, but the bed of herbs made him comfortable, wrapping him in a protective cocoon. A dark-haired Indian girl ladled water into his mouth. He drank greedily.

He had been in the jungle for three months gathering plants which might contain medicinal qualities that the University of California at San Diego hoped to use in their search for a cancer cure.

In spite of his sickness, he considered his present situation a stroke of luck. Who could know more about the medicinal properties of the local vegetation than a medicine man?

The shaman's chants rose in intensity. He made a series of strange gestures, then reached into a wooden bowl and pulled out a turtle. Its legs scrabbled at the air. When the shaman held it above Greg, he couldn't make out all of his words, but he understood most of what the priest said.

"The heart of the turtle is strong. Its spirit lives on after death. To call back the soul of my brother who wanders lost among the souls of the dead, I ask that you allow him to take on the life of the turtle."

The old man looked at Greg, his eyes searching for acknowledgement.

Greg's stomach knotted, followed by a wave of dizziness. He thought of the herbs and how they helped him, then looked up at the turtle clawing at the air. His stomach said no. His mind said yes. His gaze drifted from the turtle to the priest's. Their gazes locked and Greg nodded.

The shaman danced away making complex movements around Greg before burning a handful of herbs in the fire and kneeling on the ground. His chants settled into a low murmur. Holding the turtle at arm's length, he walked over to a stump, picked up a machete and held it next to the animal's head. The turtle retreated into its shell. The shaman raised the turtle and machete and brought them down hard on the stump as though splitting firewood.

A loud crack and the turtle cleaved neatly like a clam. The shaman jammed his fingers into one side of the shell, pulled out the crimson heart, and held it high above him.

Chanting louder, the shaman came to Greg's side and jammed the beating heart into Greg's mouth. Greg choked as the organ throbbed in his mouth like a hard, pulsating rubber ball. Salty blood ran down his throat. He inhaled through his nose and bit into the still beating mass. Its strong pulses pushed his jaws apart. The rhythm of the heartbeat filled his senses. His jaws clenched tighter and tighter, then it exploded in a wash of coppery fluid that gushed against the back of his mouth. He gagged, then swallowed, still feeling movement as the chunks slid down his throat.

They felt unnaturally warm when they reached his belly. His stomach moved with the pulses as they filled him with their insistent beat. He realized with embarrassment, that he had an erection, then he closed his eyes and let the gentle rhythm wash over him. Sleep followed.

*   *   *

He awoke feeling strong and rejuvenated. His fever had broken. He stood on wobbly legs and wandered through the village, finding a small stream running by its edge. After washing, he went back to where he'd been lying and found a huge leaf heaped with food. He ate, then fell asleep.

He lived with the villagers for the next few months, learning their language and studying their habits. The old shaman told him of the village history and shared some of his healing knowledge, but whenever Greg asked about the turtle ritual, the shaman became silent.

Greg watched him perform the rite many times and committed to memory all the herbs used, the quantity and preparation. When he was sure he understood the procedure, he approached the priest.

"You may think you know the ritual, but it would not be wise to try it," the old man said in his native tongue. "If you make the smallest mistake, the spirit cannot be appeased. The only escape is in death, and even then you must outrun the spirit's anger. Forget all you have seen."

That night the Indians put on a huge feast. Greg ate his fill and soon found himself unable to keep his eyes open until the sound of a truck and the smell of diesel jolted him awake. He opened his eyes to daylight, the jungle at his back, his gear piled beside him on the edge of a bustling jungle town. Gone were the villagers, the shaman, and the serenity of the village.

*   *   *

He went back to the university and received a hero's welcome. Nine months had passed since his disappearance and his unusual vigor from the turtle ceremony stayed with him. When the furor passed and the attention dwindled, Greg went back to his work in the Ethnobotany lab with far more insight into his work than he ever imagined.

He analyzed the herbs he collected, particularly the ones from the turtle ritual, but they showed no outstanding characteristics. He combined them exactly the way the old shaman had, and burnt them. Still nothing.

He continued working with the herbs for weeks, trying to discover any medicinal properties they might contain. Every attempt met with frustration, but he felt close, so he put in a requisition for undergraduate help.

Engrossed in his field notes one afternoon, he heard a knock.

"Come in," he muttered, not looking up from his note book.

"Dr. Friedman? I've come to apply for the lab assistant's job." The voice sounded young, female. The scent of her perfume filled him.

He peered over the top of his glasses. Big brown doe-like eyes met his. She had curly auburn hair, long, delicate eyelashes and a cute, button nose.

"My name's Sandy." She tucked a wisp of hair behind her ear and smiled. "Sandy Walker."

Greg gave her a quick appraisal. Tight jeans. Curves. Athletic. He felt the first tingles of arousal and realized that it had been a long time since he had any female contact. "What are your qualifications?"

"Biology major with a minor in chemistry."

"I see." He went back to his note book trying not to appear too interested. "Biology? Chemistry?"

"Yes." The words gushed from her.   "Specializing in   botany. More specifically rare South American species. That's why I applied. You're kind of famous. I read about how you got lost in the jungle and lived with the Indians. I'd be honored to work with you."

Greg looked up, smiling. "Report on Monday and I'll put you on for ninety days probation, then we'll do an evaluation."

"Thank you, Dr. Friedman."

*   *   *

They spent long hours in the lab working closely, analyzing his finds. Ninety days later, Greg offered her a permanent position and took her to dinner for a celebration.

They ate in silence, each sneaking peeks at the other. Sandy's hair and gold earrings reflected the rose-colored candlelight and her eyes sparkled. The two bottles of wine they drank left Greg feeling warm and aroused.

"Would you like to come back to my place for a nightcap?" he said, feeling bold from the alcohol.

"I shouldn't really…"

"Just one."

"Well -- okay."

By the time they reached Greg's, the effects of the alcohol had grown. Sandy tripped going through the front door and Greg caught her. She looked up at him, mild surprise in her eyes. He planted his mouth firmly on hers. She struggled briefly, then parted her lips, letting his tongue mingle with hers. Excitement raced through him while he pulled off her clothes, then she helped him with his. He took her in his arms and they fell back onto his couch.

"I want it," she said, spreading her legs. "Now."

The moment he entered her, he came.

Her expression cut through him. Scornful. She dressed and left without saying a word, leaving him alone with his feelings of inadequacy.

*   *   *

The next day she acted as if nothing happened and left that afternoon with no mention of the previous night, making Greg yearn for her all the more, but she remained distant and aloof.

In spite of their uncomfortableness, their work continued to show promise. The secret of the healing the shaman gave him with the turtle heart seemed to be within his grasp. The following week, he interviewed for a second lab assistant. After a number of disappointing prospects, he found Brent Stafford, another undergraduate. Though his major was zoology, his interests included botany, chemistry, and the effects of plants on the mind and body.

Aside from his impeccable academic record, Brent excelled in sports. At six-foot-two he had a thick heavily muscled torso that V'd at the waist. His dark, curly hair and mischievous blue-eyes made him irresistible to Sandy.

Greg felt jealous when his assistants grew close, but he had never had students so dedicated. He couldn't let his personal feelings get in the way of his research, so he held his emotions in check and kept his professional demeanor, but still he burned for Sandy.

He lay awake nights, thinking of her creamy thighs, aching for another chance while cursing his inadequacy; particularly in light of Brent's physique and good looks.

His somber mood hung over him and his frustration grew. He went to the San Diego Zoo to see the new tiger exhibit one day. The animals in the zoo reminded him of the jungles where he had spent so much time and it helped him to think things through. He sensed he was close to mastering the secret of the turtle heart ritual and felt confident he could duplicate it.

Two adults and two tiger cubs occupied the pit. The cubs wrestled playfully in the corner of the den behind their sleeping mother, while the adult male prowled majestically back and forth, his sleek muscles moving with fluid tension beneath his shiny coat. Greg admired the cat's grace and strength.

One of the cubs tumbled into the female, waking her. She did a long cat-stretch, then sauntered toward the male, who turned when he saw her, then circled, sniffing at her hind quarters before mounting her in a savage act of reproduction.

The cat's intensity thrilled Greg. The memory of the mating tigers stayed with him, alternating with fantasies of he and Sandy. The two images played over and over in his mind, like an out of control, repeating video.

When he thought his brain would burst, he collected the plants he needed, stopped at the biology lab for a tranquilizer gun and drove to the zoo.

Sometime after midnight he cut through a lock at one of the back gates to the tiger's den where he saw the shadowy forms of the four cats in the moonlight. Taking careful aim with the tranquilizer gun, he squeezed off four shots in quick succession.

The two adults leaped and whirled, then ran a few steps before staggering and collapsing. One cub bolted halfway across the pit and collapsed, the second ran into a corner and crouched, hissing.

Greg slipped into the pit, cornered the remaining cub and tranquilized it, then collected the darts he had shot and left the zoo with the male cub slung over his shoulder. He laid out the tranquilized cub in a secluded spot by a stream in the woods in the mountains East of El Cajon. Reciting the chants he memorized, he lit a small fire and burned the herbs he needed, performing each move precisely as he had done in his mind thousands of times before.

Chanting low, he steeled himself and slit the tiger cub, running his knife from the animal's groin to its throat. Sliding his hand under its ribs, he felt his way through the cat's entrails, finally reaching its still beating heart. The warm pulse of the organ gave him a strange thrill as his left hand closed around it.

Pushing the ribs apart, he gazed at the beating heart, exposed in the silvery predawn light. Its steady beat faltered.

Hurrying, he ripped it out with his knife, reciting the Indian prayer as he worked, then he thrust the beating mass into his mouth. The coppery smell of blood filled him while hot fluids ran down his chin onto his chest. Though larger, the cub's heart felt more tender than the turtle's. His jaws moved feverishly, devouring the meaty pulp.

When he finished, he buried the cub's remains, washed himself in the stream and drove home where he collapsed into a deep sleep.

He awoke instantly, his vision, hearing, and sense of smell acute; every sense peaked. He sat up blinking, then leaped out of bed. He felt stronger. Agile. His body sang with energy.

He spent the morning enjoying his heightened awareness, barely able to contain the energy sparking from him. When Sandy arrived that afternoon he called her into his office.

"I need to talk to you in private," he said as she came in the door. "Tonight."

"But, Dr. Friedman. It's Friday night..."

"It's very important."

She sighed. "I'll break my date with Brent."

*   *   *

"Excuse me, Dr. Friedman," she said that night as they sat together on his couch sipping their third drink. "I've been very patient. You said you had something important to talk about."

"Yes. Well um -- I've made a major breakthrough."

Her eyes lit up. "Really?" She leaned toward him. "What is it? Tell me?"

He set his drink down and rested his hand on her knee. She pushed it back and moved away. "I think you have the wrong idea."

"No." He slid closer. "You do." He put his arm up over her shoulder, then pulled her toward him.

"Don't!" she cried.

His mouth covered hers. She struggled, finally succumbing to his advances, her lips yielding to his probing tongue. His hands worked at her blouse while his tongue moved down her neck. A low moan of pleasure rose from her throat when his lips found her nipples, then she abandoned herself to passion.

His mouth danced from nipple to nipple, teasing one, then the other. She grabbed at his penis, pushing her hips toward him and pulling him toward her. Feeling all the tiger, he mounted her, thrusting feverishly, bringing her to climax after climax. When he finally came, Sandy fell back, out of breath and trembling. He carried her into his bedroom and made love to her twice more during the night, each time seeming more savage than the first. After the third time, the two collapsed, entwined in each other's arms.

Greg awoke later, hunger gnawing at his gut. He ran his tongue over his teeth. They felt sharper. The backs of his hands and the tops of his feet itched. His nails felt thicker, coarser somehow. He reached down and felt a bump on his tailbone, then opened his eyes, looked at his hands and gasped. Thick orange hairs grew out the backs of them. He kicked the blanket off and stared at his feet. Same thing.

He padded out to the kitchen, and foraged through the refrigerator for something to appease his hunger, smelled what he wanted before seeing it. His mouth watered. Raw steak. He grabbed it and tore into it with his teeth wishing it were warm.

The meat gone, he went to the bathroom and studied himself in the mirror. His eyes looked green, catlike. His crimson-smeared face

99

appeared drawn in the bathroom light. His ears looked pointed. He pulled his upper lip back and spotted two tiny fangs, then he heard Sandy.

"Greg? Greg? Where are you?"

He stumbled out of the bathroom, grabbed his clothes from the living room and let himself out the back door. He drove for hours in a panic. Between fantasies of hunting for living flesh and the ecstasy of devouring it, his mind kept going back to the turtle ritual.

He stopped at a pet store, bought a box turtle and drove back to the mountains where he performed another moonlight ritual with the turtle. When he finished, he climbed into the back seat of his car and slept.

*   *   *

When he awoke, his fingernails had returned to normal. His hands and feet looked human again. He looked at himself in the rear view mirror. His regular features had returned.

He spent Sunday recovering. The phone rang all day. He knew it was Sandy, but couldn't bring himself to answer.

On Monday morning he felt different. His back seemed to be growing hard. Like shell. He scrabbled out of bed and ran to the mirror. His eyelids looked droopy. He put his hands to his face.

He went to his office early, pondering what to do. He remembered the shaman's words and in a flash, he understood. Whatever animal he sacrificed, he would take on its form, appearance and instincts. He moaned to himself and stared at his altering fingernails. If only he could be human again.

He thought of Sandy and their lovemaking. The idea of losing her maddened him almost as much as the thought of turning into another animal. There were no animals he could sacrifice to solve his dilemma. He put his head in his hands and wracked his brain, finally looking up from his desk, frustrated.

The door to his office opened. "Good morning, Dr. Friedman," Brent said.

Greg smiled.

BRIDGE OF SIGHS

Mike stood alone in the darkness at the top of the bridge under a leaden sky that snuffed out any life the moon might have brought to the night. An icy breeze knifed through him and the chilled metal structure creaked, making the bridge sway. He took one last drag from his cigarette, flicked it into the wind and watched its orange tip spiral downward until it disappeared into the abyss below.

Pulling his jacket close, he held tighter to the suspension cable and stared down into the swirling blackness of the river, listening to the roar of the water rushing beneath him.

Three days ago they fished what was left of Liz from a tangle of tree roots at the river's edge. A plastic bag with a note to him had been pinned to her blouse.

Crazy bitch.

Only Liz would think of putting the note in a plastic bag to keep it dry. Anything to lay a guilt trip on him. That in itself had been bad enough, but the grilling the cops gave him really iced the cake. He told the same story over and over until they finally let him go.

It wasn't his fault. He'd had enough of her. Simple as that, nothing more. She threatened to do herself in hundreds of times before, but it was always the same old tired ploy for attention, like her story about the guy climbing in her window. When that one wore thin, she made a big deal about the guys hitting on her at work, then she went to her mother's to make him think she had been out with someone else.

Anything for attention.

Her constant need wore him down to the point where he felt

exhausted after spending ten minutes with her. Her every breathing moment revolved around him. He tried to get her to take up hobbies. Reading, roller blades, quilting, gardening... He spent a couple of grand on books, classes, kits, and videos, but all she wanted was to be with him.

He resented being the one responsible for her happiness. Why couldn't she find her own, then share it with him?

If he showed up a few minutes late, she'd be frantic. If he went out for a night "with the boys" she'd be hurt and jealous. Everywhere he went, she clung to him.

He had to admit, he enjoyed the attention in the beginning, but she didn't know when to stop.

"I love you," she said over and over. "I love you, Michael. You don't know how much."

She said it so many times the words lost their meaning.

"I'd do anything for you, you know that. Anything. Just name it."

The pouting followed.

"I do so much for you and you don't appreciate it."

He was tired of the same complaints.

Finally the tears came, then the guilt trip. No one knew how to lay it on thicker and better than Liz...

The wind gusted and pale moonlight broke through the cloud cover. He glanced up at the ragged wisps flitting in front of the moon, then stared down at its feeble reflection sparkling in the rushing blackness below.

What could he do now? By jumping she had freed him from the curse of being the object of her obsession. Did he love her? No, not really...

To hell with the crazy bitch. Mike turned to leave, stopped and turned back to take one last look down into the silvery blackness.

Crazy bitch, he thought, then he stepped off into the abyss.

HUNGER

(A Love Story for the Zombie Apocalypse)

E at or be eaten. That was the rule. If the hunger didn't eat him from the inside out, the others would eat him from the outside in. Cats, dogs, and scavenging rodents, all running in packs, going after the weakest; loners like himself.

So many had predicted chaos when the year 2012 hit, but all their paranoia had been for nothing — until 2050. The year that earth's last bit of rain forest extinguished and the plants, animals and other forms of life had been consumed by humans.

At first, meat had been plentiful, then life became scarce and his hunger grew, forcing him to eat anything he could find until he worshipped the same God of consumption as wolves, cats, and other predators. It grew to the point where staying in one place too long invariably brought someone or something sniffing him out, thinking him easy prey.

He climbed out from under the pile of rubble he'd been sleeping in and looked around. Broken plaster, holes in the walls, and refuse littered the floor. No roof. Through a shattered window he saw the sun low in the sky, bathing everything blood red. The day had ended. Good. Better to hunt at night.

His stomach growled. The only thing that mattered was the hunger that ran to his core. If he didn't feed it, it would feed on him.

He waited until the sky grew dark before creeping toward the street. Skeletal houses lined both sides of it, their facades weathered and battered, lawns overgrown, frames collapsing in on themselves, the same way the planet's ecology had. Broken windows stared vacantly like the eyes of so many dead.

A gibbous moon rose as he moved through the streets, past wrecked and abandoned cars with blood-spattered windows. Bits of bone lay strewn about, glinting in the moonlight. Behind the windshields, lopsided skulls grinned beside sprawled skeletons picked clean.

He ducked into one of the cars when he saw a lone figure stagger out from behind a house. A low growl came from the other side of the street and a pack of dogs burst from the darkness, yelping and bounding after the loner. One of the dogs attacked from the side, knocking the man to the ground, then the others were on him, ripping and tearing.

A short time later, one of the dogs ran off with a hand in its mouth. Another dragged something long and ragged. The sight made his own hunger kindle. He wanted to rush in and stop them, possibly catch one, but knew better. They were too fast, too many, and they could turn on him easily. He waited until the furor subsided, then continued up the street moving faster, keeping down wind, anxious to put distance between himself and the dogs.

He went a few more blocks and saw nothing. If he didn't eat soon, he'd end up food for the dogs himself. He went one more block, turned a corner and stopped.

Long atrophied synapses fired like an out of gas, sputtering engine. He stared at the buildings for a long time.

"Christina?"

The name flowed from his lips more from instinct than conscious thought -- a glimmering remembrance. Christina. Disconnected images flashed through his mind. A time before the end time. He and Christina had agreed to be together until death, but she had died early.

The details of their lives blurred into one hollow emotion that made his emptiness clamor to be filled. He walked to the end of the street and saw a low cement building with two small windows in its front. He looked at the sign above the portico.

CLEF

He tried the front door, then checked both sides of the building before finding a small window near the ground at the rear. Kicking it in, he dropped through the opening onto a hard cement floor and lay still for a moment, trying to make sense of his surroundings.

Close to silence, the only hint of sound came from the soft hum of electronics. Darkness filled his vision, except for the muted glow of red lights blinking in the blackness like so many eyes.

He rose and crept through the door to the next room. Rows of tanks lined the walls like cylindrical coffins, CLEF with a phoenix logo emblazoned on each one. More synapses fired. The control room. He hurried up the stairs.

A bank of flickering screens filled one wall, bathing the room in washed out electrical blue. One screen in the center flashed red scribbles. He remembered seeing these with Christina. Tentatively he reached out, touched the red screen and jumped backward when a man's voice filled the room.

"Emergency solar units functioning. Power conservation utility engaged." The patterns on the screen shifted and the voice spoke again. "Please select function."

Colors flashed at him. He touched one and a softer feminine voice spoke.

"Marketing presentation, section twelve. To date twenty men and forty women, twenty of them head only neuros, the other forty whole bodies, all rest peacefully in liquid nitrogen at a cool -320 degrees."

The rows of cylinders on the lower floor flashed across the screen. Wisps of white vapor floated from their surfaces. "The bodies are stored upside down in stainless steel tanks," the voice continued. "The heads placed in padded neurocans, stored in concrete vaults."

He remembered seeing and hearing this before.

"Here at the Cryonic Life Extension Facility, cryonic suspension of a head can be arranged for as little as thirty-five thousand dollars. Clients with ample resources can follow the safer route of suspending their whole bodies for one-hundred thousand dollars. Head-only patients believe their identities are preserved in their brain in the hope that future technology can make it possible for other body parts to be replaced through transplantation or cloned regeneration."

Now he understood. They were supposed to be together. He and Christina. Where was she? He touched the monitor and the screen changed. He hit it again and again, shuffling displays until a series of faces appeared. He tapped the screen a few more times, his breath catching when her face came into view.

Green eyes, deep and full of feeling. They seemed to look straight into him.

Text scrolled across the bottom of the screen.

* * * * * * * * * * * * * * * * *

STATISTICS
Christina Dixon
Location: CLEF Unit #9
Age At Time Of Suspension: 31
Cause Of Death: Auto accident
For more detailed information, please access case file # 375.

* * * * * * * * * * * * * * * * *

The visage of her soft skin and silken blonde hair stirred vague longings. His hand went to the screen of its own volition. Christina blinked from view. He banged on the monitor until a beep from the computer pierced the stillness. He put his hands over his ears as a warning message flashed in red.

* * * * * * * * * * * * * * * * *

*UNIT NINE -- DEFROST CYCLE INITIATED -- TEN SECONDS TO ABORT *
* * * * * * * * * * * * * * * * *

He stumbled out of the control room, pressing his hands to his head, hurrying down the corridors between darkened storage banks. The beep faded into the background, replaced by the low susurration of liquid nitrogen. Multicolored LED's blinked. In the middle of a corridor one of the displays flashed -300, then with quiet beeps, -298, -296. He recognized Unit # 9.

Christina.

Something clicked and white mist vented in hushed tones, its soft nitrogen whisper sounding like Christina's. The display flashed -240.

The hiss fluctuated and he swore he heard her soft sibilant voice whispering, "Do you love me?" The readout faltered and the sound of escaping nitrogen whispered again. "Do you love me?"

Christina?

He released the latch and opened the container, stumbling backward when a flood of oil spilled out. The readout stabilized at -40. Pulling himself up, he crawled to the open container.

Christina.

A thin film of oil covered her breasts, legs, hips, and hair making her smooth features look baby soft and angelic. Seeing her perfection stirred lost feelings. He removed her from the container and lovingly placed her on the floor.

"Christina."

His clothes came off. He climbed on top of her, kissed her pale cheek and felt the longing flood through him. Reaching down, he took her cold fingers in his.

He couldn't contain himself any longer.

He pressed his lips to hers, his tongue hungrily exploring the recesses of her mouth, then he pressed his lips to the side of her face and sank his teeth into the soft skin of her cheek.

CRASH DIET

Jimmy sat in his beach chair at La Jolla Shores, tipping a cold one, resting it on his pot belly between sips while half a dozen gorgeous babes pranced in front of him, nimble as deer; every one of them, Southern California, beach-bunny perfect. Definitely built for speed. Silken blonde hair fluttered in the breeze as a long legged blonde sprang toward a volleyball. Sculpted muscles slid beneath smooth, tawny skin as she lunged and missed. The ball bounced past her, rolling to a stop beside Jimmy.

There was a God.

Jimmy picked up the ball and waited for her to trot to him. When their eyes met, he lost himself in two crystal clear, blue pools of serenity that left him speechless. Her delicate features couldn't be any prettier. "Whoa," he said, shaking his head and tossing her the ball.

"Thanks." She caught it and tucked it under her arm. Luscious grapefruits stood straight and firm above a trim midriff that flared out to gently curving hips. The cut of her snow white bikini offset her tanned skin. San Diego's finest. No question.

"What's the whoa for?" she said.

"Sorry. Don't mean to be rude and I'm not feeding you a line, but you are the most beautiful creature I have ever laid eyes on."
She graced him with a stunning smile. "You're kinda cute yourself." She sighed. "If you only took better care of yourself."

"What do you mean?"

She pointed to his stomach. "That little beer table's not very attractive. Too bad. You really *are* cute."

He looked down at his gut and felt his face flush. He couldn't believe what she had said. He should have been pissed, but the way she had said it stopped him. Not mean. Sincere.

He looked back up and saw a smile in her eyes.

"Doesn't have to be that way," she said before turning and running back to the volleyball game, then calling over her shoulder. "If you really want to do something about it, I can show you how."

He sat dumbfounded. Not only had she shot him down, she had offered to help. He watched her cute butt wiggle back to the volleyball net and closed his eyes, imagining himself alone with her in a hot tub, sipping wine and massaging each other. He felt a stirring in his groin and stopped himself. It was embarrassing enough when she pointed out his gut, but if she busted him with a woody...

He opened his eyes again and saw that the volleyball game had ended. The goddesses sat together, heads close in intimate conversation, followed by telling glances in his direction. Part of him wanted to march over and straighten them out, but one look down at his gut stopped him. What the hell would he say? If she was sincere about helping him, she had to be sincere when she told him he was cute.

The beauties rose like a flock of graceful birds taking wing, fluttering down to the water, leaving the blonde behind. She looked over at him, smiled, then laid back on her blanket.

This is it, Hot Shot, Jimmy told himself. If that ain't an invite, you're a fat, worthless slob. He drained his beer, stood, sucked in his gut and walked over to where she lay.

She opened her eyes when he approached and smiled up at him.

"Hi," he said. "I never had anyone talk to me like that. What you said wasn't very nice, but I sensed your sincerity. You really think you can help me?"

Her smile broadened and her clear blue eyes sparkled. God how he wanted her. "Does that mean that you'd go out with me if I was in better shape?" he asked, feeling stupid, but not caring.

"That's a distinct possibility," she said, still smiling. She patted the sand beside her. "Have a seat."

Not believing his luck, Jimmy dropped down next to her.

"My girlfriends and I are really into taking care of ourselves."

"That's an understatement."

Another flash of perfect teeth. "We're on a special diet that increases lean body mass, burns fat and gives us more energy than we ever had before. It will make you feel so good, you won't want to drink beer or anything. You'll end up looking great and feeling good."

"You're all on it?"

"We were out of shape like you until we started the diet, then in a few short months we had great shapes and more energy than we knew what do with."

"What do I have to do?"

"Come to a meeting."

"Like one of those Weight Watchers things?"

"Oh no," she said emphatically. "I tried everything in the past, but nothing worked -- until I found VitaLife."

"VitaLife?"

She reached into her beach bag, pulled out a card and handed it to him.

He took it and read.

VitaLife Consultant -- Terri Miller

"Call me," she said. "We're meeting this Tuesday night at 7:00."

He thought he detected the salesperson in her. Maybe she was playing him for a sucker, trying to get him into some silly marketing bullshit. "I'm not sure if I can make it."

"That's all right if you want to stay out of shape and miss out on something great." She smiled once more, winked, and closed her eyes. No doubt about the tone of her last comment.

A challenge.

*   *   *

VitaLife had a small, modern office building tucked away in a cul-de-sac amidst acres of gleaming, modern high-tech businesses in La Jolla. Jimmy slipped in the back door of the small auditorium at ten past seven. Terri had declined his offer to pick her up, saying she had to be there early to help get things ready. He hoped she might go out for coffee afterward.

He took a seat in the back, scanning the crowd, hoping to see her. As soon as he sat, the mostly full hall erupted in applause and a tall, healthy looking, silver-haired man strode to the podium beaming a smile to the enthusiastic crowd. His eyes had the same clear sparkle as Terri's. The tanned, smooth skin of his face made him look way too young for a man with silver hair.

He held up his hands, stilling the applause. "Hi, I'm Seth Johnson, founder and CEO of VitaLife," he said in a TV announcer voice. "If you've never been here before, welcome to the VitaLife family. We want to be your family for life."

Jimmy felt as if he stumbled into a religious revival.

"We want to show you how to be fit and healthy using the most amazing breakthrough in nutritional technology. Through its state of the art, rigorously controlled, secret processes, VitaLife has brought your health into the next millennium. All from natural organic sources."

Jimmy half-listened to Seth's spiel about growth hormones, bio availability, Inulin analogs, cancer, heart disease, strokes, fiber, and cholesterol, all the while scanning the crowd for Terri, finally spotting her front row, center, looking up at Seth like an adoring teenager love struck by a rock star god. Her cadre of volleyball beach beauties lined up beside her. Same expressions.

Another round of applause filled the room and people scattered throughout the audience went up to the podium, each giving their own testimonials. All of them wore badges that said:

I CAN SHOW YOU HOW.

"I lost forty pounds of fat in two months and got off of three different medications," a robust sandy-haired man said. "Thank you, VitaLife."

"I lost nine inches off of my hips and fifty pounds in my first three months," said a dark haired, well-proportioned, middle-aged woman. "Now I date men half my age and they still can't keep up with me."

Titters ran through the audience followed by brief applause.

"Thank you, VitaLife," she said.

Toward the end, Terri and her beach bunny babes, each came to the podium with their own horror stories of obesity, anorexia, and bulimia. Every speaker had a healthy glow, and all had the same, crystal clear sparkle in their eye.

When the last of the babes left the podium, Seth stepped up again and announced, "Please join us for a complimentary VitaLife shake. Guaranteed to give your body all the vitamins, minerals, and nutrition it needs -- without the fat. Thank you for coming."

Another round of applause filled the room, then people started toward the back of the hall where trays of shakes and glasses had been set out on tables. Jimmy pushed through the crowd, going against the flow to find Terri.

He spotted her up front in animated conversation with Seth. When he got close her eyes flashed recognition. She smiled, then came to him, taking him by the hand. "I want you to meet Seth," she said, pulling him along.

The silver haired man turned toward them, flourishing a smile.

"Seth, I'd like you to meet Jimmy," Terri said. "Seth's the one that started all this."

"Pleased to meet you," Jimmy stuck out his hand. Seth gave it a firm shake while his eyes searched Jimmy's. Jimmy felt as if Seth's steady gaze took in everything there was to know about him.

"It's a pleasure to know you," Seth said in a rich baritone. His gaze darted briefly to Jimmy's stomach. "VitaLife's going to do a lot for you." He smiled, glanced at Terri and winked at Jimmy.

"Think he'll make it to the winner's circle?" Seth asked.

"I just met him," Terri said. "I'm hoping to get him signed up on VitaLife's In-Shape system."

"Is that right?" Seth said enthusiastically.

Jimmy couldn't believe his ears. He looked at Terri, sensing eagerness behind the pleading look in her eyes. This was real important to her. Was it because she cared for him?

After drinking one of their shakes, Jimmy left the meeting with four cans of VitaLife chocolate and vanilla shake mix, and a video. He had to admit, it did taste good.

"One shake in the morning and one in the afternoon," Terri told him. "Stick with it and you'll see results quick."

"When can I call you?"

"Give the VitaLife a couple of weeks, then we'll go out."

*　　　*　　　*

After a few days of shakes, Jimmy slept more soundly than he had in years, waking with fragments of weird dreams that he couldn't quite remember. Twice a day, he filled his blender with milk, a banana, and a scoop of the VitaLife. He found himself craving the smoothies more each day.

While blending his shake one day, he licked his fingertip, dipped it in the VitaLife and stuck it in his mouth. An explosion of flavor made his mouth water. Take and eat of this, for it is good, he thought, turning off the blender.

He poured the smoothie into a tall glass and drank it, savoring the refreshment. That night he couldn't wait to get home and drink his second one. He slept deep, waking up feeling refreshed and looking forward to his morning smoothie; this time half-remembering Terri in his dreams.

In the first week, he felt his energy level increase like a plane taking off. By the weekend he lost two inches off his gut and had so much energy, he started lifting weights and running. Fat dropped from his body like melting butter and his muscles felt strong and grew defined. He could swear that his eyes had begun to take on the same clear look Terri and Seth had.

Toward the end his second week, he was almost out of VitaLife, so he called the number for the reorder desk on a Thursday night.

"Good evening, VitaLife," a sweet sounding, feminine voice said. "How may I help you?"

"Hi, I'd like to reorder one can of chocolate and one can of vanilla VitaLife."

"Your membership number?"

"Membership number?"

"You don't have one?"

"I'm afraid I don't. I'll give you my Visa number and we'll put it on the plastic."

"Who's your sponsor?"

"Sponsor? I don't have a sponsor. I just want to buy a couple of cans of VitaLife."

"You'll need a sponsor, then we'll sign you up for auto- reorder so your VitaLife can ship automatically at the end of each month and debit your credit card."

"I'm not so sure I want to do that. I'll just put these two on the plastic for now."

"Sorry sir, that's against policy."

"I'm trying to buy some of your product here. Spend some of my hard-earned American green. What do you mean, it's against policy?"

"Didn't your sponsor -- I mean who gave you your VitaLife in the first place."

"Terri."

"Terri Miller?"

"She's one of our greatest success stories. There's obviously been some misunderstanding. Let me take your name and number and I'll give her a call for you."

Jimmy stifled a surge of anger. This was bullshit. He gave the girl the information and hung up. Ten minutes later, she called back, all apologies. She took his credit card order, promising him it would ship the following day. He ran out of shake mix Friday night and woke up missing his morning smoothie on Saturday.

By Saturday afternoon his craving grew, so he went to the store and bought a can of Slim-Fast, but it only upset his stomach and left him craving VitaLife even more. As the day wore on, a headache started at the back of his skull until he couldn't bear it any more.

After a night of fitful, sweaty sleep, he awoke to a pounding head that six Excedrin made bearable, but did not extinguish. He tried drinking Slim-Fast again, but it only upset his stomach, so he tried regular food, which he promptly vomited.

Chills set in. He knew he was coming down with something, so he crawled into bed and tossed and turned, one moment miserable from sweats and chills; the next, agonizing over his twisting gut and pounding head. He somehow managed to sleep on and off through the afternoon and night. When he did dream, he dreamed of drinking VitaLife smoothies.

*   *   *

He opened his eyes to sunlight. He had missed work, but didn't care. No way was he going anywhere feeling like this -- except to the doctor. Stumbling out of bed on shaky legs, he went to the kitchen for water and found himself going to the front door where he found a box of VitaLife. He hadn't even heard the UPS guy.

On impulse, he opened the box, cracked open a can of VitaLife, grabbed the scoop and dumped the white powder straight into his mouth. His stomach calmed and his body relaxed, making him feel heavy. His headache diminished. He climbed back into bed and let sleep take him, opening his eyes hours later in total darkness. Fragments of an erotic dream drifted in his mind like fading smoke. He remembered something vaguely sexual with Terri, but with Seth there. In his room?

His heart jumped when the phone rang. Putting his hand to his chest, he took a deep breath to calm himself, then fumbled in the dark, finding the phone by the sound of the ring.

"Hello?"

"Did you get your order?" Terri said.

"Finally. What's with this sponsor shit?"

"I'm sorry, there was a mix-up in the paperwork. Give me your credit card number and we'll get you on automatic reorder. It'll debit your account every month and your VitaLife will be on your doorstep at the same time every month. Let's get this over with so we can make some plans for a date."

"A date?" Surely she wasn't holding this credit card shit over his head for a date. Did she have any idea of what he had just been through? He took stock of himself. Other than feeling a little groggy, he felt okay -- but he did crave more VitaLife.

"This is the best way to get your VitaLife," she said after he gave her the number. "No worries. It'll be there for you all the time. Just like I will. You won't have to go anywhere to get it. It'll come to you."

"Yeah, you're right," he said giving in, thinking about the smoothie he was going to have as soon as he hung up.

"Let's get together Saturday night," she said softly.

"What time should I pick you up?"

"Meet me at VitaLife."

"VitaLife?"

"We'll talk when I see you there. We'll go out after."

"Oh. Okay."

"See you then."

He hung up, went to the kitchen and made a VitaLife smoothie, savoring its sweetness and the growing feeling of satisfaction that he felt after drinking. Best one he ever had.

The rest of the week passed on a regular routine, two VitaLife shakes a day and a small meal at night. He felt better with each passing day. His energy level increased and he actually felt lighter. Looking at himself in the mirror one morning, he was pleasantly surprised to see that his gut had shrunken and his eyes had some of the sparkle that he had come to think of as the warm glow of health that Terri, Seth, and the other VitaLife people had. What would she think of him now?

*   *   *

"Jimmy, you look wonderful," Terri said, when she saw him. She gave him a warm hug. Her perfume insinuated itself into his mind and went straight for his lower parts. "Look at you." She made a show of stepping back and giving him the once over with her clear blue eyes before giving him a seductive wink.

"I've been sticking with it," Jimmy said, a little embarrassed by her attention.

"How do you feel?"

"Great."

She gave him a wet kiss on the cheek and pinned an

I CAN SHOW YOU HOW

button to his shirt, then she took him by the hand and led him to the front row. Everyone greeted him with smiles that told him how lucky he was to be with her, but he wasn't sure he was ready to sit through another sales pitch. She sat him front row center, beside her. In spite of all the hoopla, he realized that the important thing was that he was with her. Now.

The childlike yearning that he saw in her eyes when Seth stepped up to the podium sealed his fate. Her rapt expression told him how much this meant to her. Shit, if it was that important, he could suffer through another "Ra! Ra!" session, then he could have her all to himself. "So where do you want to go to after this?" he heard himself saying.

A pained expression pinched her pretty face. "I'm sorry, I just found out that I have to stay late for a Winner's Circle meeting."

His heart dropped. "Tonight? You mean you don't want to go out to dinner?"

"Shhhsh," she said, dropping her voice to a whisper. "We'll talk about it after Seth's talk." She turned away and put her full attention on Seth, who spoke his usual homilies with liberal doses from his hundred watt smile. Terri listened, leaning toward Seth, as if taking sustenance from each word that he spoke.

Jimmy did a slow burn, not hearing the words, feeling that she had somehow tricked him. Was she going to go out with him or was she stringing him along to get him hooked on this stupid VitaLife Church of the Almighty American Greenback? He had to admit that he saw spectacular results in a short period of time, but if she was going to play him like this just to get him into the sales program, he might as well date a hooker. At least then, he knew what the deal was up front.

The sound of applause shook him from his reverie and to his horror, he realized that they were applauding him. Terri pushed him to his feet, smiling up at him, a dreamy look on her face. He looked around, feeling cornered by the sea of smiles. He waved to them and sat back down. His skin felt hot and prickly and his face burned from embarrassment.

"Jimmy's an inspiration to us all," Seth said. "I'll just bet you he'll be in the center of the Winner's Circle in no time." He smiled and winked at Terri. "Now if you'll join us in the back, we'll be serving complimentary VitaLife smoothies."

"Come on," Jimmy said while they moved with the crowd toward the back of the hall. "Let's sneak away. You can miss one meeting."

Come out with me."

Her eyes grew wide. "I'm sorry, Jimmy, but I cannot miss a Winner's Circle meeting. I'll call you toward the weekend. I promise."

"Yeah fine, you do that," he said, feeling his hurt flare into anger. "Go to your meeting. I wouldn't want you to miss that." He pushed past the people in front of him, leaving Terri behind and kept going when he reached the door, ending up in the parking lot sitting in his car. Simmering. He slouched down in the driver's seat, torn between leaving and waiting for her to come so he could have another word with her. Maybe he had overreacted.

People drifted out of the VitaLife building, first in trickles, then en masse, filling the parking lot with the sounds of car doors closing and engines starting. The lot emptied quickly, leaving Jimmy set off from a small group of cars parked across from him. Terri's was one of them.

Jimmy crossed his arms and waited until the lights winked off around the building. What the hell was going on? Had there been a power outage? Not likely. An outage would have extinguished them all at once.

The whole building lay in darkness and people were still in there -- unless they had left by another door. Why would they do that? He thought. And where would they go without their cars? Better make sure everything's all right.

Half way around the building he saw a flicker of orange glinting behind the mirrored window. Pressing his face to the glass, he saw the blurry forms of people gathered in a circle in a large, dimly lit room. Dozens of candles burned on the perimeter. What the hell were they doing in there?

He walked the length of the building searching for a way in. Around back he found a steel door beside a shipping dock. He let himself in and worked his way down darkened hallways, past offices and rooms full of lab equipment, listening intently while heading in the direction of the circle of people.

Close to where he figured they'd be, he heard murmurs, so he slowed, letting the voices guide him until he found himself outside a heavy door with a fire escape latch bar. He leaned down until the bar bottomed out, pressed his shoulder to the door and eased it open a crack to peer into the room.

The first thing he saw was Terri's bare ass. He'd know it anywhere. He gazed longingly for a few more seconds before scanning the rest of the people, seeing that they too were nude. What the hell was it? Some kind of orgy?

They held hands, eyes closed, faces suffused with the soft glow of orange from the candle light, serene expressions filling their faces. Each and every one of their bodies, both male and female were perfect and beautiful, each with their own unique beauty; like a pantheon of immortal Greek Gods and Goddesses.

They parted, revealing the withered and emaciated remains of something that looked vaguely human. Flaps of powdery gray skin clung to its skull like some grotesque patchwork puppet face. Ragged chunks of flesh and tendon hung in strips from the bones of its skeleton. Powder white bones stuck up from its rib cage like tusks in an elephant grave yard. The stomach and innards appeared to have collapsed into a white powder that lay under everything like fine Caribbean sand.

Jimmy's first thought was that he saw a wax figure which had to be part of some bizarre parlor game, until the circle turned into a line that started beside the corpse. Seth stood on the other side of it, hands spread as if in benediction. "Take and eat of this, for it is good," he said.

Everyone in line knelt before the body, one at a time. Seth mumbled something to each of them, then dipped a small silver ladle into the pile of powder beneath the ribs and spooned it into the kneeling supplicant's mouth.

∗   ∗   ∗

Jimmy could barely remember leaving and had no recollection of his drive home. Only the terror. The first thing he did when he got in the house was to flush all his VitaLife down the toilet. Next he locked the doors and windows, pulled all the shades and took the phone off the hook.

His first cravings came after midnight; a tiny gnawing in his gut. He drank a Budweiser to quell it, but the beer only made it worse, so he tried eating. Nothing agreed with him and his craving grew worse along with the beginnings of what he knew would be a blinding headache.

After downing a handful of aspirin he crawled into bed, craving VitaLife more by the minute while his body threw its own tantrum; fever, chills, stomach and muscle cramps, interspersed with fits of vomiting and diarrhea. Three times, he picked up the phone to order, finally deciding to give in.

An operator picked up on the second ring. "Good evening, VitaLife," the sweet sounding, feminine voice said. "How may I help you?"

"I need some VitaLife."

"Your membership number?"

"I don't know it, but I'm a regular customer. I'll give you my Visa number."

"Who's your sponsor? We'll sign you up for auto-reorder. You won't have this problem."

"Terri Miller."

"I'll get in touch with her and get this straightened out, then I'll call you right back."

"But I -- hello?"

He punched in the number again, getting a busy signal. He slammed his cell phone down.

The night wore on, passing into morning until he slipped into a fever-sweat delirium, losing track of time while drifting in and out of consciousness, never escaping the pain. Every joint in his body ached and his skin hurt if he touched it. Even his bones seemed to scream in agony.

The walls, the floor, his closet and especially his sheets and blankets came alive like dozens of serpentine monsters, some wormlike, others closer to snakes, writhing in and around him. Sickly pink and green slithering insects crawled over his face and down his back. One worked its way up his nose. Two giant fanged snakes burrowed into his gut, sucking the soft, fleshy entrails from his torso with loud slurping sounds. He felt the tugging as a physical pull deep inside him until darkness took him.

*   *   *

He woke up in daylight with the damp sheets entwined with his body. His head throbbed and he felt weak. He had no strength and his body looked swollen and bloated, as though someone had pumped him full of cottage cheese. His beer belly stood out more prominent than ever and his skin looked like someone had dusted him with talc.

The phone lay inches from his face. With great effort in what felt like an eternity, he managed to call VitaLife, reaching what sounded like the same sweet sounding operator, once more getting no further than the need to sign up for auto-reorder. Looking down, he watched with detached fascination as the fingers of his left hand crumbled into white powder. He thought of his feet, but could not feel them. The light in the room seemed to grow brighter and he heard voices. Terri's.

Seth's.

As he drifted into oblivion, the last thing Jimmy heard was the sound of Seth's voice saying, "Take and eat of this, for it is good. It is the flesh of a new and everlasting covenant."

Jimmy licked his lips, at long last tasting the powder that had become the sweetest nectar he had ever known.

Take and eat of this, for it is good, he thought with his dying breath.

And it was.

ABOUT THE AUTHOR

Matthew J. Pallamary's historical novel of first contact between shamans and Jesuits in 18th century South America, titled, **Land Without Evil**, was published in hard cover by Charles Publishing, and has received rave reviews along with a San Diego Book Award for mainstream fiction. It was chosen as a Reading Group Choices selection. **Land Without Evil** was also adapted into a full-length stage and sky show, co-written by Agent Red with Matt Pallamary, directed by Agent Red, and performed by Sky Candy, an Austin Texas aerial group. The making of the show was the subject of a PBS series, Arts in Context episode, which garnered an EMMY nomination.

His nonfiction book, **The Infinity Zone: A Transcendent Approach to Peak Performance** is a collaboration with professional tennis coach Paul Mayberry that offers a fascinating exploration of the phenomenon that occurs at the nexus of perfect form and motion, bringing balance, power, and coordination to physical and mental activities. **The Infinity Zone** took 1ˢᵗ place in the International Book Awards, New Age category and was a finalist in the San Diego Book Awards. It has been translated into Italian by **Hermes Edizioni.**

His first book, a short story collection titled **The Small Dark Room Of The Soul** was mentioned in The Year's Best Horror and Fantasy and is presently being translated into Portuguese. His second collection, **A Short Walk to the Other Side**, published by Mystic-Ink Publishing was an Award Winning Finalist in the International Book Awards, an Award Winning Finalist in the USA Best Book Awards, and an Award Winning Finalist in the San Diego Book Awards.

DreamLand a novel about computer generated dreaming, written with Ken Reeth was also published as an e-book by Mystic-Ink and won an Independent e-Book Award in the Horror/Thriller category and was an Award Winning Finalist in the San Diego Book Awards. It is presently being translated into Italian and Portuguese.

Eye of the Predator was an Award Winning Finalist in the Visionary Fiction category of the International Book Awards. ***Eye of the Predator*** is a supernatural thriller about a zoologist who discovers that he can go into the minds of animals. His quest for the truth leads him into a murky world of magical plants and ancient shamanic rituals that ultimately bring him face to face with the enigmatic mystery of his past.

CyberChrist was an Award Winning Finalist in the Thriller/Adventure category of the International Book Awards. ***CyberChrist*** is the story of a prize winning journalist who receives an email from a man who claims to have discovered immortality by turning off the aging gene in a 15 year old boy with an aging disorder. The forwarded email becomes the basis for an online church built around the boy, calling him CyberChrist.

Phantastic Fiction - A Shamanic Approach to Story took 1st place in the International Book Awards Writing/Publishing category. ***Phantastic Fiction*** is Matt's guide to dramatic writing that grew out of his popular Phantastic Fiction Workshop. It incorporates elements of shamanism that have formed the basis for Joseph Campbell's legendary Hero's Journey. Through his research into both the written word and the ancient beliefs of shamanism, Matt has uncovered the heart of what a story *really* is and integrated it into core dramatic concepts that have their basis in shamanism.

Night Whispers was an Award Winning Finalist in the Horror category of the International Book Awards. Set in the Boston neighborhood of Dorchester, ***Night Whispers*** is the story of Nick Powers, who loses consciousness after crashing in a stolen car. He comes to hearing whispering voices in his mind. When he sees a homeless man arguing with himself, Nick realizes that the whispers in his head are the other side of the argument. This ties in with a federal investigation investigating a series of macabre murders that point to a druid cult that appears to be connected to the same homeless shelter that Nick is led to. It is being translated into Italian.

His memoir ***Spirit Matters*** detailing his journeys to Peru, working with shamanic plant medicines took first place in the San Diego Book

Awards Spiritual Book Category, and was an Award-Winning Finalist in the autobiography/memoir category of the National Best Book Awards, sponsored by USA Book News. ***Spirit Matters*** is also available as an audio book. It is slated to be translated into Norwegian.

Matt's work has appeared in Oui, New Dimensions, The Iconoclast, Starbright, Infinity, Passport, The Short Story Digest, Redcat, The San Diego Writer's Monthly, Connotations, Phantasm, Essentially You, The Haven Journal, The Montecito Journal, and many others. His fiction has been featured in The San Diego Union Tribune which he has also reviewed books for, and his work has been heard on KPBS-FM in San Diego, KUCI FM in Irvine, television Channel Three in Santa Barbara, and The Susan Cameron Block Show in Vancouver. He has been a guest on the following nationally syndicated talk shows; Paul Rodriguez, In The Light with Michelle Whitedove, Susun Weed, Medicine Woman, Inner Journey with Greg Friedman, and Environmental Directions Radio series. Matt has also appeared on the following television shows; Bridging Heaven and Earth, Elyssa's Raw and Wild Food Show, Things That Matter, Literary Gumbo, Indie Authors TV, and ECONEWS. He has also been a frequent guest on numerous podcasts, among them, The Psychedelic Salon, and C-Realm.

Matt has received the Man of the Year 2000 from San Diego Writer's Monthly Magazine and has taught a fiction workshop at the Southern California Writers' Conference in San Diego, Palm Springs, and Los Angeles, and at the Santa Barbara Writers' Conference for twenty five years. He has lectured at the Greater Los Angeles Writer's Conference, the Getting It Write conference in Oregon, the Saddleback Writers' Conference, the Rio Grande Writers' Seminar, the National Council of Teachers of English, The San Diego Writer's and Editor's Guild, The San Diego Book Publicists, The Pacific Institute for Professional Writing, and he has been a panelist at the World Fantasy Convention, Con-Dor, and Coppercon. He is presently Editor in Chief of Mystic Ink Publishing.

WWW.MATTPALLAMARY.COM

BOOKS BY MATTHEW J. PALLAMARY

THE SMALL DARK ROOM OF THE SOUL

LAND WITHOUT EVIL

SPIRIT MATTERS

DREAMLAND (WITH KEN REETH)

THE INFINITY ZONE (WITH PAUL MAYBERRY)

EYE OF THE PREDATOR

NIGHT WHISPERS

CYBERCHRIST

PHANTASTIC FICTION

A NOTE FROM THE AUTHOR

I would like to give special acknowledgement to Barnaby and Mary Conrad, the founders of the Santa Barbara Writer's Conference, as well as Paul Lazarus, Charles (Chuck) Champlin, Jonathan Winters, Gayle and Dennis Lynds, Charles (Sparky) Schulz, Sid Stebel, Abe Polsky, Phyllis Gebauer, Walter Halsey Davis, Cork Milner, Shelley and Anne Lowenkopf, and especially Joan Oppenheimer, who took me under her wing at a critical time in my career. All of these caring souls started off as my mentors, and soon became beloved colleagues.

I also want to give thanks to Michael Steven Gregory, otherwise known as MSG, and Wes Albers, not only solid friends, but as the driving forces behind the Southern California Writer's Conference where I have been teaching writing workshops for as long as I have been teaching at the Santa Barbara Writer's Conference.

Thank you too, to Monte Schulz for saving and resurrecting the Santa Barbara Writer's Conference and to Nicole Starczak for running the show, and for keeping the SBWC vital and alive.

In a very short period of time, I became the youngest workshop leader at the SBWC and remained so for fifteen years, adopted into a wonderful extended writing family, treated like a son and a favored nephew by such amazing, legendary, nurturing talents.

I found myself in this position in a large part due to the envelopes I pushed with my writing and the otherworldly themes and elements I embraced following the trail blazed by Ray Bradbury, a major influence in my writing and in my life.

Ray was one of the best short stories writers who ever lived.

Thanks to my friend, colleague, and mentor Sid Stebel, I was lucky

127

and blessed to get to know Ray as a friend and mentor through the SBWC, which Ray kicked off for thirty five years.

A few years before he left us, I was honored to be asked to write a piece for a limited edition hard cover tribute to Ray, so in honor of the inspiration, blessing, and support I received from him as well as everyone else in my extended writing family to carry on the storytelling tradition, I am reprinting the original essay here and publishing this eclectic collection as a tribute to Ray Bradbury, short story writer extraordinaire.

A RAY OF LIGHT

In the early seventies I read a short story in a high school English class titled **There Will Come Soft Rains** that captured my imagination in a way that few stories could. Its opening burned an indelible image into my mind the same way the outlines of a family had been burned into the side of a computerized house where robots went through preprogrammed computerized chores in the aftermath of an atomic blast. This post apocalyptic family portrait created by Ray Bradbury still haunts me more than three decades after first reading it.

In the years that followed I discovered that I had a knack for writing, but never in my wildest imaginings did I think I would actually become a writer, and never in my even wilder imaginings could I conceive of knowing Ray Bradbury as a guiding light, an inspiration, and a loving, caring mentor.

In nineteen-eighty-eight I attended the Santa Barbara Writer's Conference for the first time, and on opening night I heard Ray kick off the conference with an outpouring of love, passion, and inspiration, not only for the written word, but for life in general.

"The hell with everything else", he exhorted. "Write for the love of it!"

Year after year I returned to the conference, first as a student, then as a workshop leader, each time hearing this same message spoken in different ways with just as much passion, if not more, and each year my inspiration was rekindled anew.

In nineteen-ninety-four I published my first short story collection titled **The Small Dark Room of the Soul.** Friends and colleagues urged me to ask Ray for a blurb because we were affiliated through the conference, but I found myself in mortal terror at the thought of it.

Eventually I screwed up my courage and asked the advice of Sid Stebel, a friend, mentor, and a close friend of Ray's. Sid went to bat for me and eventually Ray blessed me with the words: "Bravo More!"

Never in my life had two simple words carried so much power.

Six years later when my first novel, **Land Without Evil** came out, I was once again urged to ask Ray for his blessing. During that time he suffered a major health setback that hospitalized him, so I gave up all hope of getting another blurb. To my amazement, soon after my request I received a typed yellow card signed by Ray, full of encouragement, apologizing for not getting back to me sooner, saying he couldn't read my work, but giving me permission to use his original blurb. I treasure that card and have it framed and displayed prominently in my writing space beside a picture of Ray and me. I consider myself blessed to know him personally and doubly blessed by the wish he granted me.

Cinderella had her fairy godmother to inspire her with loving light beyond her wildest imaginings, and I have my own Ray of light, a writing godfather who did the same for me.

Made in the USA
Middletown, DE
14 June 2017